D0182810

Damascus
Nights

Rafik Schami

Translated by Philip Boehm

ARABIA BOOKS

LONDON

This edition first published in Great Britain in 2011 by

Arabia Books
70 Cadogan Place,
London SW1X 9AH
www.arabia-books.com

Copyright © 1989 & 2011 Beltz Verlag, Weinheim und Basel
Programm Beltz & Gelberg, Weinheim

English translation copyright © 1993 by Farrar, Straus and Giroux. Inc.

Originally published in German as *Erzahler der Nacht*

Published in the USA by Interlink Books,
an imprint of Interlink Publishing Group, Inc.

ISBN 978 1 906697 35 8

Printed and bound by CPI Group (UK) Ltd, Croydon, CR0 4YY

A CIP catalogue for this book is available from the British Library

CONDITIONS OF SALE
All rights reserved. No part of this publication may be reproduced,
stored in a retrieval system, or transmitted in any form or by any means,
electronic, mechanical, photocopying, recording or otherwise, without
the prior permission of the publisher.

This book is sold subject to the condition that it shall not, by way of trade
or otherwise, be lent, re-sold, hired out or otherwise circulated without the
publisher's prior consent in any form of binding or cover other than that in
which it is published and without a similar condition including this
condition being imposed on the subsequent purchase.

Damascus
Nights

How
Salim the coachman
arrived at his stories
without ever leaving his seat

It's a strange story to say the least: Salim the coachman
lost his voice. If it hadn't happened right before my
very eyes, I would never have believed it. Everything
started in 1959, in August, in the old quarter of Damascus. Even if I wanted to make up such an incredible story, Damascus would still be the best place to
set it. Nowhere but Damascus could such a tale take
place.

In those days, many strange people lived in Damascus. But what's so strange about that? They say when
a city has been lived in continuously for over a thousand years, its citizens inherit the accumulated eccen-
tricities of ages past. And Damascus can look back on
several thousand years. So you can just imagine the
kinds of unusual people running up and down its
crooked streets and alleys. Old Salim the coachman
was the most unusual of them all. He was short and
slight, but his deep, warm voice easily made him seem
a large man with broad shoulders, and he was a legend
in his own lifetime, which doesn't mean that much in

Leabharlanna Poibli Chathair Bhaile Atha Cliath
Dublin City Public Libraries

a city where legends and pistachio pastries are but two of a thousand and one delights.

What with all the coups during the fifties, it was not unheard of for residents of the old quarter to confuse the names of statesmen and politicians with those of actors and other celebrities. But no one ever made any mistake about Salim the coachman, who lived in the old town and who could tell such stories as would have his listeners laughing, or weeping, or both.

Among the unusual people running up and down the city, there were many who had a suitable saying ready for any occasion. Yet there was only one man in Damascus who could produce a *story* for *everything* —whether you had cut your finger, caught cold, or fallen tragically in love. But how is it that this coachman Salim became the most famous storyteller in all Damascus? The answer to this question involves, as you may have guessed, another story.

In the 1930s, Salim worked as a coachman, driving between Damascus and Beirut. Back then the journey took two exhausting days. And they were two dangerous days as well, because the road wound through the rugged Great Horn Gorge, which was crawling with brigands who earned their daily bread waylaying travelers.

The coaches themselves differed little in appearance. They were constructed of iron, wood, and leather and carried four passengers. The competition

for business was merciless; often it was the hardest fist
that decided who would drive, and the passengers had
no choice but to climb out of one carriage, pale with
fright, and board the coach of the victor. Salim fought
as well, but rarely with his fist: he used his cunning
and his invincible tongue.

When the Depression came to Syria, fewer and
fewer people could afford to travel, and good Salim
had to devise some way to provide for his family—he
had a wife, a daughter, and a son to feed. What's
more, robberies were on the rise, since many impov-
erished farmers and tradesmen were fleeing to the
mountains to earn their bread as highwaymen. Salim
would quietly promise his guests: "If you ride with
me, you'll make it through without a scratch, and so
will all your money and your bags." His good relations with the robbers enabled Salim to make such
promises. Again and again he would drive from Damascus to Beirut and back unmolested. Whenever he
entered a bandit's domain, he would leave a little
wine by the side of the road, or else some tobacco—
but secretly, so the passengers didn't notice—and the
robbers would give him a friendly wave. He was
never attacked. But after a while, the secret of his
success trickled out, and all the other coachmen
began to imitate him. They, too, left gifts by the
roadside and were allowed to pass in peace. As Salim
said, it got so that the brigands turned into fat, lazy
collectors, utterly incapable of inspiring fear.

Thus his guarantee of a journey safe from robbers soon lost its unique appeal and Salim wondered desperately what to do. Then one day an old lady from Beirut came to his rescue. During the ride, he had recounted in great detail the adventures of a robber who had fallen in love with none other than the sultan's daughter—Salim was personally acquainted with the man. When the coach reached Damascus, the old woman is said to have shouted, "May God bless your tongue, young man. Time flew much too quickly in your company." Salim called this woman his "good fairy" and from then on he promised his clients he would regale them with stories the whole way from Damascus to Beirut (or Beirut to Damascus) so that they wouldn't even notice the hardships of the journey. This was Salim's salvation, for no other coachman could tell tales as well as he.

But how did the old fox—who could neither read nor write—always come up with a fresh story? Quite simple! After his passengers had heard him tell a tale or two, he would ask them casually, "Now perhaps one of you would like to treat us to a story?" There was always someone, a man or a woman, who would answer, "I have a story that's absolutely unbelievable, but I swear to God it really happened." Or else: "Well, I'm not very good at telling stories, but a shepherd once told me one, and if you promise not to laugh at me I'll be glad to give it a try." Naturally Salim encouraged all his passengers to tell their sto-

ries. Then he would spice them up and pass them on to the next travelers. In this way he always had a fresh and inexhaustible supply.

The old coachman could charm his listeners for hours on end. He would tell of kings, fairies, and highwaymen—he had experienced much in his long life. Whether the stories were happy or sad or full of suspense, his voice held everyone spellbound. Not only could it evoke sorrow, anger, and joy, it could even make you feel the wind, the sun, and the rain. Whenever Salim began to speak, he would soar inside his stories like a swallow. He would fly over mountains and valleys, and he knew every road, from our little side street all the way to Peking, and back. Whenever he so desired, he would land on Mount Ararat—nowhere else would do—and smoke his waterpipe. And if the coachman didn't feel like flying, he would streak through the seven seas like a young dolphin. And because he was shortsighted, a buzzard accompanied Salim on all his travels and lent the old man his eyes.

Small and frail as he was in real life, in his stories he not only subdued giants who boasted glaring eyes and frightful moustaches, he also beat sharks into retreat and on almost every journey he would wrestle with a monster.

Salim's flying around the world was as familiar to us as the graceful gliding of the swallows across the blue Damascus sky. How often as a child did I, too,

stand by the window and soar in my thoughts like a swift above our courtyard. Those flights hardly ever frightened me back then. But I would shiver along with everyone else at Salim's battles with sharks and other monsters of the deep.

At least once a month the neighbors asked the old coachman to tell the story about the Mexican fisherman, a story Salim especially enjoyed. It went something like this: Salim was swimming in the Gulf of Mexico, as peacefully and happily as a dolphin, when a giant evil octopus attacked a tiny fishing boat, causing it to capsize. The octopus started to wrap its tentacles around the fisherman, and he would have been squeezed to death if Salim hadn't rushed to his aid. The fisherman was so overjoyed he wept and swore by Holy Mother Mary that if his pregnant wife bore him a son he would name the boy Salim. Here Salim would always pause to check whether we were listening closely.

"And what if it had been a girl?" someone was bound to ask. The old coachman would smile contentedly, puff on his waterpipe and stroke his gray moustache. His answer was always the same: "Then he would have named her Salime, of course."

The struggle with the mighty octopus was a long one. In winter we children would huddle in Salim's room, shivering with fear for the coachman who was

battling the octopus with its countless suckers, and if it happened to thunder outside we would huddle even closer.

Tamim, one of the neighborhood children, had the obnoxious habit of grabbing me by the neck with his fat fingers in the middle of the story. That would scare me every time and I would scream. Then Salim the coachman would quickly reprimand the troublemaker, ask me where he had left off, and return to his battle with the giant octopus.

Afterward, every little rustle of fallen leaves would give us goose bumps, as if the octopus were lying in wait for us. Tamim, that chicken, who had acted so unimpressed while Salim was telling the story, was more afraid than anyone else. He lived a few houses down, you see, so he had to cross our courtyard and walk through a dark alley to get home. But three other children and myself lived in the same house as Salim, and we felt his reassuring nearness even at bedtime.

One night the octopus was especially ferocious. I was overjoyed to reach my bed safe and sound. Suddenly I heard Tamim's voice, whimpering softly at the old man's door: "Uncle Salim, are you still awake?"

"Who goes there? Tamim, my boy, what's the matter?"

"Uncle, I'm afraid. Something's growling in the dark."

"Wait, my boy, just wait! I'm on my way. I only have to unsheathe my Yemenite dagger," reassured Salim through the closed door.

Tamim waited, ashamed, since all of us who lived nearby were laughing out loud.

"Keep one step behind me, and, even if a tiger jumps us, don't be afraid—I'll hold him back," Salim whispered and brought Tamim to safety, even though the old coachman was half blind and could barely see in the dark. No one could tell lies as well as Salim.

Yes he loved to lie, although he had no patience for exaggeration. One day a neighbor had joined us and was happily listening to the story of the octopus and the Mexican fisherman. But then, right in the middle of the battle, he insisted on knowing how long the octopus's tentacles were.

Salim was startled by the question. "Very long . . . with hundreds of suckers," he said somewhat confused.

"How long? One yard? Ten yards?" scoffed the neighbor.

"How should I know? I didn't go there to measure his arms. I had to get rid of the thing, not tailor it a suit," Salim snapped back, and we all laughed. The

man kept mumbling something to himself while the coachman beat the octopus until it vomited its whole supply of ink and fled. But as soon as the battle was over—just when Salim was preparing to smoke his well-earned waterpipe on a sandy beach in Cuba— the man interrupted a second time: "So it was you who colored the oceans blue!"

"No, no, the oceans were blue long before I was born. Many brave souls fought with many octopi. The first one to do so lived three hundred and twenty-seven years before Adam and Eve," remarked the coachman unperturbed and gave his waterpipe a couple of pulls. Then he returned to the coast of Cuba to recuperate.

I once asked Salim how it was that his words could put people in such a spell, and he said, "It's a gift from the desert," and since I didn't understand what he meant, he explained: "The desert, my friend, seems beautiful to strangers at first. People who only visit it for a few days, a few weeks, a few months, find it enchanting, but in the long run life in the desert is tough. It's hard to find anything beautiful in the scorching heat of day or the screeching cold of night. That's why no one really wanted to live there, and so for a long time the desert was very lonely. It cried out, but the caravans just passed on by, happy to escape the barren wilderness unharmed. Until one day my great-

great-great-grandfather, who was also named Salim, was crossing the Sahara with his tribe. He heard its cries for help and decided to remain, so as not to leave the desert all alone. Many laughed at him for giving up the green gardens of the city to seek his fortune in the sands. But my great-great-great-grandfather stayed true to the desert. His whole life long he believed that paradise was simply loneliness that had been overcome. From then on, his children, and his children's children, drove away the desert's loneliness with their laughter and games, and with their dreams. The hooves of my great-great-great-grandfather's horses drummed the desert's limbs awake, and the soft gait of his camels brought it rest. In gratitude the desert gave to him, and to all his children, and his children's children, the most beautiful colors in the world: the secret paint of words, so that they could tell each other stories by campfire light and on their endless journeys. And so my ancestors made sand into mountains and waterfalls, into ancient forests and into snow. By the campfire, in the middle of the desert, almost dead from hunger and thirst, they told stories of a paradise flowing with milk and honey. And they took their paradise along on all their travels. Their magic words made every mountain and valley, every planet and every world lighter than a feather."

In over forty years Salim never drove his carriage beyond Beirut, but on the wings of his words he traveled the globe like no one else. So when it

happened that he of all people suddenly lost his voice,
the whole neighborhood was bewildered.
Not even his best friends
could believe
it.

2

Why
a strange disquiet
interrupted the hitherto quiet
comings and goings of seven gentlemen

If Salim had listened to his father he would have become a happy merchant or craftsman like each of his five brothers, but he was determined at all costs to be a coachman. In those days the profession had a very bad reputation: coachmen were generally considered no better than rowdy drunkards. Nevertheless Salim took an unusual pride in his vocation.

Apart from his gifts as a storyteller—a profession that enjoyed a better, if blander reputation than coachman—Salim was favored with yet another talent: he could make wounded swallows fly again, and this, indeed, was no mean feat. Salim's neighbors were puzzled by his relations with the swallows, and they quarreled among themselves over the source of his gift. Some proclaimed that his hands were blessed; others accused him behind his back of some sort of wizardry. It was this magic, they concluded quietly and not without some fear, that enabled Salim, and Salim only, to restore flight to any swallow. Most adults, however, thought the whole thing a swindle.

Those glorious gliders, whose graceful flights

adorned the sky above Damascus, nested underneath our roofs. Time and again we would find a swallow that had somehow fallen out of its nest flapping helplessly on the ground. And of course it's a well-known fact that swallows refuse all nourishment so long as they cannot fly. Had it not been for Salim the coachman they would have died of hunger. We children would carry the swallows to him—and, as I said, to him alone—and he would drop everything, take the quivering bird into his large hands, and walk out onto the balcony. What he whispered to the bird there, and why he kissed it, was his secret. No one else knew how. He gave back to the skies their best acrobats. The swallow would race away, sometimes thanking the old man with an elegant loop above his head.

People didn't know much about Salim. He seldom spoke about himself. And when he did, it was so much like one of his stories that no one really knew whether he was talking about himself or one of his heroes. People frequently referred to Salim the coachman, but I bet most of them couldn't even tell you what his last name was. As a matter of fact, it was Bussard.

The Bussard family belonged to the nomads of the Arabian desert. Following a failed uprising against the Ottoman sultan in the eighteenth century, the clan was dispersed and resettled. Salim's grandfather was held in a Damascus prison until his death; after that the family was not allowed to leave that city. Salim's

father learned the art of tanning and prospered in that trade. His oldest son took over the small tannery; two others traded in leather goods. One son became a tailor. Another became a goldsmith but died of small-pox at an early age. Salim, the youngest, was named after his great-great-great-grandfather. From earliest childhood he was restlessness personified and caused his parents more trouble than all his five brothers combined. Occasionally he would disappear for weeks or months on end, only to return in rags and laugh himself silly at the punishments his parents would then impose. Instead of learning a trade, he spent his time running errands for the coachmen. From one caravanserai to the next he made his way across Arabia, Turkey, and Persia. It was even ru-mored on the street that he had spent a year in Mo-rocco as an apprentice to a master of black magic. Salim himself would just laugh slyly whenever any-one asked; but he knew more about the habits and habitations of the Moroccan Berbers than any teacher of geography.

For thirty years Salim earned his bread as a coach-man. When his son later emigrated to America and his beautiful daughter left with her wealthy husband to settle in the northern part of the country, Salim lived alone with his wife in a small room. In contrast to his beloved son, who sent letters but not a single dollar, Salim's daughter provided her parents with a

small allowance. Old coachmen were not eligible for pensions.

Salim's wife, Zaida, was an unassuming person. She lived a quiet life. It was only after her death that Salim's neighbors discovered what a fiery and courageous woman she had been. Once she had disguised herself—as Salim told the story—as a black horseman and rescued him from seven armed soldiers who had come to conscript him. All the neighbors agreed that Salim had never served in the military—but no one could imagine little Zaida scaring off seven soldiers.

Every evening seven friends came to call on the old widower. They were all the same age, about seventy. A locksmith named Ali was the biggest among them; he was so big he practically took up the entire sofa. The last to join the old gentlemen had been the geography teacher, Mehdi, and although he had been coming for eight years, the others still referred to him as "our newcomer." Musa, a short and plumpish barber, was the only one in the group who still attempted to disguise his seventy years by dyeing his hair. The most elegant of the friends was the former statesman Faris. Shortly after Syria had gained independence he became minister of finance, and his radical reforms had earned him the popular nickname "the Red Pasha." Tuma, the fifth member of the

circle, was known as "the emigrant" even though he had returned from America over ten years before. Junis, the café owner, was the only one of the gentlemen to whom all were grateful. It was in his coffeehouse that they had come to know one another over the years—Salim and Ali were the only ones who lived on the same street. For years they had gathered at the café: it was far and wide the only place you could sip a genuine Yemenite mocha and smoke a proper waterpipe. But ever since Junis' son had transformed the old-fashioned, Middle Eastern café into a flashy, modern bar, none of them went there anymore.

The seventh member of the group was a small man named Isam, who had served twenty-four years in prison for a terrible murder he did not commit. By chance, the true murderer was caught one year before Isam was to be released. For a man seventy years old, he was incredibly restless, as if he wanted to use his remaining years to make up for the time he had lost in prison. From Monday to Thursday afternoon he pulled a small cart loaded with vegetables through the city's more remote neighborhoods. At the Friday market he traded in songbirds. Saturdays and Sundays he sold toasted chickpeas in front of the movie houses.

Salim liked Ali the best. The locksmith said very little, but he enjoyed listening. He was the perfect complement to the talkative coachman; although he

scarcely spoke, he would laugh at the slightest provo-
cation. But that wasn't all. Salim praised Ali as the
bravest man in the neighborhood. In the early forties
he supposedly boxed a French general on the ear in
the middle of the street. At the time the country was
under French occupation. People say he did it because the general was drunk and making fun of the
Prophet Mohammed, who forbade all alcohol. Ali
didn't like to talk about it. But Salim the coachman
described the general's terrible revenge in detail. He
had Ali arrested and taken to a barracks outside Damascus. There they forced a gallon of red wine into
his stomach with a funnel, then bound him to a stake
in the scorching sun. When Ali lost consciousness the
soldiers dragged him out of the barracks and dumped
him in a ditch by the side of the road. A pea-
sant family that was passing by found him and took
him in. Naturally they didn't know what was wrong
with him, since they had never heard of alcohol poi-
soning. But the old woman gave him a mixture of
olive oil, yoghurt, and vinegar to make him vomit
and in that way saved his life. Ali had to spend several
days in bed at their house before he regained his
strength. Meanwhile his family had learned of his
arrest and had gone to the barracks to ask his whereabouts. All they received there was the cynical reply,
"He's not here, maybe he's with the Prophet." When
Ali had finally recovered his strength, he was too
ashamed to return home. He made his way to a

certain nightclub and waited a long time outside for the general to appear, then gave him a terrible beating. It was a wonder the man survived. Ali had to flee to the mountains, where he stayed until the French left the country four years later. Only Salim the coachman knew his whereabouts and secretly brought him food, clothing, and the latest news week after week.

The seven friends met every evening without exception. Whether it was raining or the Army was staging a coup, they arrived just before eight and didn't leave until after midnight. If one of them was sick and couldn't attend, his wife or a grandchild or a neighbor's child would bring a detailed explanation. Colds and similarly lame excuses didn't count.

I was the only child in the neighborhood whom the coachman allowed to stay when the old men arrived. In return I often had to play errand boy. This wasn't always the nicest of jobs, since the old men were so forgetful. The emigrant often forgot his tablets and sometimes his glasses, the café owner his snuff, and the former minister more than a few times forgot his elegant handkerchiefs—and no others would do. Sometimes I had to run these annoying errands in the rain, and their houses were scattered all across the city. Only coachman Salim never sent me anywhere. But he did once make me cross my heart and swear to him that I would never reveal a single

word I had heard in his room. I swore by the soul of my grandmother Nadjla, whom I loved more than all the saints together, that I would keep every word to myself. But apart from Salim's nosy neighbor, Afifa, no one cared what the old men were talking about anyway; and besides, I never would have told anything to her, that two-legged radio station, even if she had tempted me with chocolate.

Now and then I had the feeling that the old men sent me out just so they could speak their minds a little more freely. I acted as if I didn't understand why one of them would ask me to fetch tobacco for the third time that day or why someone else would request a second tablet only an hour after he had asked for the first. Faris, the former statesman, was the worst. He could sneeze at will, whenever he so pleased, and completely fill his handkerchief with snot. Once outside I would dawdle underneath the window and eavesdrop on their secret stories, which usually began: "Now that the boy is gone . . ."

The seven friends came every day. Over the years their visits became one of the thousand customs of our neighborhood. No one, not a single person, paid them any mind as they made their way to old Salim's. Their comings and goings were as much a part of our daily life as the children's shouts and the chatter of the swallows that filled the sky above our street each evening. All of this changed abruptly when Salim the

coachman lost his voice. Yes, Salim, the man whose magical words transformed his room into an ocean, a desert, or a jungle, was suddenly struck dumb.

Overnight the mute coachman became the only subject of conversation in the neighborhood. People now followed the movements of the old men with a curious interest—a stranger might even say, with reverence. Knowing my own street as well as I do, though, I seriously doubt whether its inhabitants have ever felt real reverence for anyone. But the fact remains: people were curious. To tell the truth, the whole neighborhood was completely intrigued by Salim's strange silence. I myself was worried sick.

From then on I went to visit him every day
and there was no one who could
make me
leave.

3

*How
the old coachman
lost his voice and made
his friends the talk of the town*

People in Damascus refer to the last month of summer as "flaming August." By day the city swelters in a state of permanent fire alarm, as the temperature climbs to over a hundred and four degrees in the shade. What's a measly fan supposed to do with heat like that except swirl the hot air, hopelessly, around and around and around? In other months things cool off once the sun has set, much to everyone's relief, but not in August. The earth stays hot even at night, and the mercury seems stuck at eighty-six degrees, so that people can barely sleep. And only an hour after sunrise the temperature again begins to soar.

One night in August 1959, Salim suddenly awoke, bathed in sweat. Sitting up in his bed, he sensed that someone else was in the room. "Who's there?" he asked.

"I was wondering when you'd wake up," a woman's voice answered, somewhat relieved. It was dark as pitch, but the coachman could feel the woman's delicate hand touching his face. She smelled of orange blossoms. "I have come, my dearest friend, to say goodbye."

"What do you mean, goodbye! Who are you?" asked Salim, since he had never heard the voice before.

"I am your good fairy, the one who has breathed life into your dusty, wooden words and made them grow into a magical tree of tales. Do you really think you could have told stories as long as you have if I hadn't been standing steadfast by your side for over sixty years? How many times have I had to pick up wherever and whenever you lost the thread? You are beyond all doubt the best storyteller in Damascus, but now and then you've gone a little too far, and boxed yourself in so badly with all your subplots and digressions, you forgot which story you were telling. Especially when you rescued the Mexican fisherman. Even though you've told that story three hundred times, you're always so taken by your own victory over the octopus that you forget you were really on your way to Cuba to fetch the black pearls you needed to save the princess. And while you were relaxing and smoking your waterpipe, I was so nervous I was shaking—until you finally found your thread again and told your listeners how you discovered the black pearls and finally managed to rescue the princess, and then returned with her to Damascus, where the story began. It was often exhausting, but it made me happy to bring your heart a smile of relief.

Those were hard years of labor with you, my friend!"
The woman paused a moment. "Now, just like you,
I have grown old and gray and am ready to retire. But
when I do, you will lose your voice. I've always loved
you, Salim. Your voice and your hands have always
tickled my heart like a little feather. Which is why I
have asked the fairy king for a special favor, which he
has granted. He listened to what I had to say and
laughed: 'Yes, yes, I know you've always been in love
with that funny coachman of yours, haven't you?
Well, go and tell him our one condition.' "

"Condition? what condition?" The coachman's
throat was dry.

"After that question you have only twenty-one
words left. Then you will become mute. However
. . . if you receive seven unique gifts within three
months, then a young fairy will take my place and
stand by your side. She will release your tongue from
silence and you will go on telling stories until your
dying day. You will be able to box yourself in as
much as you want—she's very young and can easily
keep up with you.

"Don't squander your words, Salim, my beloved.
Words are responsibility. Ask me nothing more.
You'll have to discover the gifts for yourself; the fairy
king didn't even tell me what they might be. Consider carefully whatever you want to say, you have
only twenty-one words left!"

Salim the coachman, molded as he was by the

ancient customs of Damascus, never in his life considered any offer final nor any price written in stone.
"Only twenty-one words?" he whispered in a voice
that would have softened the hardest seller's heart.

"Now it's only eighteen," the fairy reprimanded
him; and opening the door, she disappeared in the
darkness. Salim sprang out of his bed and hurried after
her. Just then a neighbor came hurrying out of his
room, heading for the toilet. "Good God, it's hot!
You can't sleep either, Uncle?" he asked the bewildered coachman.

"No," Salim replied and cursed himself for having
wasted another word. The whole night he paced up
and down his little room, constantly looking out his
window until morning broke. He made himself some
tea, thoughtfully chewed a piece of bread, and when
the clock of the nearby church tower struck eight, he
left his room with tired steps. The neighbors wondered at his bad mood; the coachman didn't even
return their greetings: "May your day be happy and
blessed!"

Salim paused outside the door of his house. Two
street sweepers were passing by; one was sprinkling
water out of a great leather bag he carried on his back,
to keep as much dust as possible from swirling up, but
the little droplets simply rolled like tiny dust-covered
marbles into the many troughs and gorges of the
narrow street. The second man was following the
water-sprinkler with a gigantic broom. Step by step,

he worked his way forward through the dust. Salim waited until the air behind the two street sweepers had cleared and slowly trudged off to his friend Ali. The locksmith lived a few houses down the street.

Salim knocked on the door and waited. After a short while, a little girl cracked the door slightly and stole a peep at the old coachman. "Uncle Salim!" she shouted into the house as she opened the door and ran inside. Fatma, the locksmith's plump wife, hurried to the door, apologizing for her granddaughter's shy behavior and inviting their friend inside. To her amazement, however, he simply stood there, waving his hands and resisting her insistent invitation. "But Salim, what's wrong with you? Ali's still in bed—our little Nabil has a fever, though even when he's healthy he likes to crawl into bed with his grandfather every morning."

Salim signaled that he would wait at the door until his friend came. It was difficult for him to explain to the woman that he mustn't talk and carelessly waste what few words remained. It was even more difficult for the woman to understand the old man, whose thrashing about made him seem odder than ever. Finally both heard the clatter of the locksmith's wooden shoes, and down the length of the hallway the big man's voice bellowed, "What's this? My Salim's as shy as a young bride today?" He laughed when his wife whispered to him on her way inside that something was wrong with Salim. "Go and put the coffee on the fire. He's just waiting for me to invite him in. And that's the way it should be, too!" Ali looked at his friend with a broad smile and was even more puzzled than his wife had been when Salim declined his invitation. Without saying a word, Salim desperately tried to explain that the locksmith absolutely had to come to his place that evening.

After a while Ali understood his friend's gesticulations. But no matter how hard he tried, he couldn't figure out why Salim was bothering to stress the obvious, and above all why he wasn't speaking.

It was even harder for Salim to explain to his other friends that they, too, should not fail—under any circumstances—to come to his house. By the time he had completed his difficult mission, it was nearly noon. He ate a piece of bread and some olives and lay down for an hour to recuperate from the strain of his morning's tour of the old part of town.

Early that afternoon the seven friends had already gathered at Salim's. Full of concern for their friend's sanity, they sat together and stared at the old coachman, who calmly proceeded with the rites of the meeting. First he poured the tea, then, as courtesy demanded, he passed the freshly prepared waterpipe to the oldest in the group, the emigrant.

"So, what's the matter with you, brother Salim?" The former statesman broke the silence.

Salim spoke very slowly. In seventeen words he recounted what the fairy had said. He wanted to add that he didn't believe it himself, but he couldn't get another word across his lips. Even when the barber tickled him and tweaked him and Salim wanted to laugh and cry he couldn't produce a single sound. His face turned pale and he clutched at his throat.

All of a sudden Ali the locksmith cried out, "I know what the seven gifts are. For years we've been coming here, drinking him out of house and home, smoking up his room, and not one of us fools has ever even thought of having him over. Seven invitations are what will free his tongue! And I can assure you: once he tastes my Fatma's baked eggplant, he's going to sing like a canary. So tomorrow we'll meet at my place," the locksmith said and hurried home.

On his way out, Ali was relieved to see that Salim was smiling. But Faris, the former minister, read Salim's smile more as a peculiar sort of smirk. On the way home he voiced his suspicion to Musa, the barber, and was quite surprised to discover the latter shared his doubt.

"It's not that the old coachman's game is so crude," said the barber, lighting a cigarette. "What's sad is that the others were so easily taken in. All grown-up men, and they turned pale as a sheet. Did you see how Tuma kept crossing himself and crying out, 'Holy Mary, have mercy on us!'? But how can we unmask him? I tweaked him so hard an elephant would have screamed, but he didn't even squeak."

The minister had always had the greatest respect

for the clever barber, and it wasn't the first time they shared the same opinion. "No, tweaking's not going to get us anywhere," he agreed.

The two went on walking for hours. They looked for a quiet café where they could sit down with a waterpipe and talk as long as they liked. In each of the three cafés they entered, the radio was blaring away at full volume. Since February of 1958, Syria had been united with Nasser's Egypt. From its inception, this United Arab Republic seemed to live on the brink of disaster. That particular day, President Nasser was broadcasting a three-hour-long harangue against the regime in Iraq, which had turned overnight from bosom friend to archenemy. The people were sitting glued to the radio, listening to his fiery words.

"The presidents are talking more and more, and the people are saying less and less," said Faris, disgusted, and slammed shut the door of the Glass Palace.

"Just listen to those words!" the barber gushed once they were back on the street, where the president's voice was sounding from the windows of the shops and houses. "What are books compared to that! What is the most beautiful writing compared to the divine sounds of the human voice? Mere shadows of words on paper!"

"Please, don't exaggerate," Faris replied and waved his hand. "Writing is not the voice's shadow but the tracks of its steps. It is only thanks to writing that we can listen to the ancient Greeks and Egyptians even today, that we can hear their voices as full of life as if they had just spoken. My friend, only writing has the power to move a voice through time, and make it as immortal as the gods."

"But you have to admit, Nasser does have a damned good larynx. Whenever I hear him I get goose bumps and my eyes start welling up with tears." Musa stubbornly stuck up for the president.

"You're right about that," answered Faris, "and there is the problem."

The two men walked on slowly, discussing Nasser, whose incessant talk made only the former minister suspicious, and Salim, whose sudden silence had raised the suspicions of both. They wondered how they could unmask the sly old coachman.

The next day the seven friends met at Ali the locksmith's. The eggplants were indeed indescribably delicious. Salim ate with pleasure and thought about his wife, Zaida, who used to cook so well. Ali kept refilling his friend's plate with one slice of eggplant after another. "So do you like it?" he asked. Salim smiled and nodded his head, but didn't say a word.

"Nothing against your wife's culinary accomplishments," said Mehdi, the teacher, "but when Salim tastes my wife's tabbouleh salad, together with some ice-cold arak, then you'll see, he'll outtalk Scheherazade herself. As you know, my wife is Lebanese, and no one makes tabbouleh salad like the Lebanese."

The next day, the silent coachman savored the magnificent salad along with some cool arak. Salim overdid it, as was always the case with things he enjoyed; that night he drank so much he got drunk, and ate so much he suffered from severe flatulence.

For six nights in a row the friends fed their Salim. Every day he grew a little fatter, but still, he didn't say a word.

Early in the morning on the seventh day, Faris, the minister, was beaming. Less out of love for his guest than because he was so sure of himself. When his friends came over, everyone—except Musa the barber, Faris' fellow conspirator—was amazed at the huge roast mutton, and even more at the numerous bottles of beer lying in a large bowl of ice. "In heat as hellish as this, there's nothing better than ice-cold German beer," the minister said enticingly. "It's something completely different from the soapy water we make here that people mistakenly call beer."

"I don't drink alcohol," grumbled Ali.

Tuma the emigrant, a self-proclaimed connoisseur, praised the fine taste of the minister who spared no cost in serving his friends such expensive imported beer. "Even in America," he attested, "people know of German beer."

Junis, Mehdi, and Isam followed Tuma's lead, even though they didn't care much for beer. If being a guest in Damascus means being flattered and treated like a king, it also means subscribing to the sacred, unwritten law that the king must keep silent and gratefully accept anything and everything his generous host may serve. Salim smiled and partook of both roast and beer. And although he had never tasted the bitter drink, he soon grew to like it.

During the course of the evening, even Ali took a few swallows out of sheer curiosity. For his part, Salim emptied one bottle after another, and shortly after midnight he was snoring in his seat.

Ali the locksmith laughed out loud. "He still can't talk, but he sure can snore like a walrus just as he always did!"

Faris, who had only been sipping at his beer, gave a wink to the barber, who yawned audibly—as if he had been waiting for his cue—and said, "Let's go home. It's getting late!"

"And Salim? What about my friend Salim?" Ali roared angrily.

"Don't worry about your friend. He'll be fine spending the night here with me," said the minister.

It was very late when the six old men left their host's spacious, well-kept garden. Salim was snoring loudly in the large guest bed. It sounded as if a sheep were fighting for its life in a deep, foamy sea of beer.

Faris looked grim as he entered Musa's apartment shortly after ten the next morning. "I'm going to keel over if you don't make me some coffee," he said.

Musa ran to his youngest daughter in the kitchen, asked her to make some strong coffee, and hurried back as fast as he could to the anxious old minister. "I spent the whole night crouching beside his bed. He was snoring ferociously, and when I whispered to him, 'Salim, Salim! Shall I make you some coffee? Salim are you asleep?' he didn't answer. Then I tried to scare him, as we had agreed. I turned on the light and yelled as loudly as I could, 'Get up! You're under arrest!' He jumped up, then he just smiled at me and went back to bed. I was boiling over with rage. Why was he smiling? I was exhausted and struggling to stay awake. Painful as it was, I kept my watch until dawn, when I fell asleep in my armchair. Now my neck's as stiff as a board. But it all wouldn't have been so bad if he hadn't peed."

"Peed?" Musa was amazed but could not suppress a giggle. "Surely not in bed?" he added.

"Even that wouldn't have been so tragic. No, I was deep asleep, dreaming about a brook, when suddenly I heard it begin to murmur. I opened my eyes and there he was, standing in the corner, peeing into the pot of my rubber tree. Explain that to my wife! She's been nursing that tree for years."

The two men drank their coffee, deep in thought, and late in the afternoon they trudged over to Salim's. They were almost ashamed when they entered the small room. Salim was merry but not even that could cheer them. They drank their tea slowly and waited for all the members of their group to arrive. The last one there was Ali the locksmith. He was pale and scolded the minister for having seduced him into drinking German beer. Faris, in reply, only whimpered softly that he had meant well.

"And why did you scare Salim in the middle of the night?" Junis asked Faris.

The minister was more than a little surprised at the question.

"Salim acted out for me what kind of nonsense you were up to during the night," explained the coffeehouse owner.

The minister looked at Salim, but the latter just smiled peacefully and shook his head.

"Yes, that was our plan," said the barber, stepping in to save his fellow conspirator. "We thought that the fairy might have scared Salim so much that his tongue went lame. My mother—God have mercy on her soul and on the souls of your own ancestors— used to say, 'It takes a fright to scare a fright.' We wanted to loosen his tongue with a powerful shock. Once I had a neighbor, a very young and beautiful woman, and one day her husband just up and died. The woman was very sad, and she went to the cemetery every day, to kneel at the grave of her husband and tell him what she had done that day, or cooked, or bought. One afternoon she went to the graveyard. She was exhausted from her housework and soon fell asleep in the shade of a tree. When she woke up it was pitch-dark. She became very frightened. She wanted to run out of the cemetery when suddenly a cold hand grabbed her. Then a ghastly voice croaked: "Where are you going?" The woman flailed about and ran like the devil all the way home. Believe it or not: she was struck dumb, and half her hair turned white as snow, as if by a spell. Try as they might, three doctors failed to help her. Finally my mother said that what the woman needed was another good scare— then she'd be able to talk again. The widow was instructed to visit her husband's grave at night, to tell him in her heart what had happened and ask him to repay her true love with a word to Saint Thomas, who could heal her. Saint Thomas, as you know, was very curious, and curious people know more about tongues than anyone else. So that evening, just as the sun was setting, the woman made her way to the cemetery. Her heart trembled as she thought what she wanted to ask her dead husband. Suddenly a deep, angry voice came roaring out of the grave: 'What do you mean—Saint Thomas? Leave me in peace and don't bother me with your Saint Thomas. You know very well I couldn't stand nosy people when I was alive. I don't want him pestering me here in heaven. And you, just get the hell out! Let me enjoy my death in peace! If you don't want to enjoy your life, then come and join me in my grave!' With these words, a hand came out of the ground and reached for the woman. She screamed like mad and ran away as fast as she could go. She was cured and went on to live a very satisfying life."

When the barber had finished his story, the minister nodded thoughtfully, and in his heart he was grateful to this fast-talking barber.

"I know!" exclaimed Junis. "It's seven wines. Our Salim has to drink seven wines to untie his tongue. I know from many years' experience in the coffeehouse that wine loosens the tongue. And you can bet that the men who wound up talking my ear off were always the ones who had first sat as silent as stones in the desert."

As if the suggestion had come from heaven and not the mere mortal Junis, the barber and Faris smiled at each other. "That's it!" they cried out in an unrehearsed chorus.

Night after night the old men wandered from one establishment to another. Convinced that wine was what was needed to unknot Salim's tongue, they drank away until the sun began to rise.

Gradually the neighborhood began to mutter about the old men's nocturnal expeditions. The locksmith's wife, Fatma, was especially helpful in furthering this talk. Her exaggeration knew no bounds: the innocuous pubs of the old quarter were transformed into mysterious places in the new part of town, where young women danced stark naked, bathed in a seedy, dim red light. Naturally Fatma didn't forget to make her neighbors swear not to betray this secret. But that's the way neighbors are in Damascus, they have tongues like sieves; they couldn't keep a secret if they wanted to. And rumors, well, they're strange creatures with a will of their own: the more colorful they grow, the more their true origins fade.

By the end of this futile treatment, Salim felt as if he had been completely leached and bleached. His old headaches, which he had all but forgotten since he stopped drinking so much, once again began to batter his brain.

The barber next suggested that they have Salim sniff seven different perfumes—every bottle seven times. He knew for a fact that the tongue is closely tied to the nose.

With the first bottle, Salim was visibly pleased as he inhaled the refreshing aroma. It also happened to be his favorite scent, orange blossoms. The second bottle emitted the pleasant odor of carnations, but he only sniffed halfheartedly. With the third bottle—rose water—he was merely performing his duty, and after five whiffs of the fourth flask, which contained essence of jasmine blossoms, he was ready to quit. His friends, however, forced him to undergo the entire therapy, with the result that the old coachman acquired yet another headache—but not his voice.

Seven shirts and seven trousers did as little to free the old coachman's tongue, as did an astonishing pilgrimage to eighteen officials. For years Salim had tried to obtain a government pension; his application had always been rejected. Yet now he carried his completed forms to eighteen offices, without uttering a word, and eighteen officials smiled at him and stamped their stamps on his papers with unheard-of alacrity. As soon as he reached the second office, Salim was convinced he had made some mistake, but then the third civil servant loudly wished him an enjoyable retirement.

In Damascus, officials never stamp that quickly, and never ever do they deign to smile. The stamp is a piece of every official's soul, and if he has to press it down on a sheet of paper, it hurts his soul—though a banknote or two has been known to lessen the pain. Smiles, and on top of that, good wishes for a retirement underwritten by the state—that, for Damascus, was a miracle.

Now, it isn't easy in Damascus to find a miracle that all the inhabitants can actually agree on. That's one of the remarkable things about this ancient city. Over its thousand years, Damascus has witnessed thousands of marvels—false prophets, alchemists, magicians, and more—but the Damascenes themselves believe in only one true miracle: the one that is brought about by having the right connections to the right official.

The former minister had carefully lubricated the way so that Salim would receive approval of his pension application without any friction and without a word being said. And Salim couldn't believe his eyes when the friendly lady at the state bank handed him one hundred seventy-five liras. He was so moved he started to cry—but still, he didn't say a word.

The seven friends gathered at Salim's in a modest celebration of the newly acquired pension. Salted pistachio nuts graced the table in addition to the daily tea. The minister basked in the praise the other men were bestowing on him. Only Tuma, the emigrant, seemed pensive.

"What's the matter with you?" asked the barber.

"Nothing. Tomorrow—tomorrow I'll tell you my idea," Tuma whispered curtly. His voice sounded weary, as if his thoughts were a burden.

4

Why
one proposal
made Salim happy but
caused his friends to quarrel

It was a little past eleven when the seven old gentle-men headed home. In the large courtyard the neighbors sat in small clusters, enjoying the fresh September night. A few men were playing cards next to the pomegranate tree; across the courtyard some others were hovering over a backgammon board. A group of women had collected around Afifa in front of her door.

Salim carried the empty glasses and the teapot into the kitchen, rinsed them off, and hurried to his room.

"Uncle Salim, come join us!" Afifa called out with a note of pity.

"No, he should come here and teach this beginner how to play backgammon," said one of the players, a plump man with the squeaky voice of a child.

"You're just lucky," his opponent lashed back. "You call that playing? If I'd had just one of your throws, you'd have run to your wife long ago—to cry on her shoulder."

Salim stopped for a minute, gave the backgammon players a nod, smiled, and walked back to his room.

He turned off his light and sat down on the sofa. He was not tired.

The old coachman still couldn't grasp how Faris, the minister, had managed to bring such a hopeless case to such a successful conclusion. He took out his wallet, removed the bills, gave them an approving sniff, and put them back. For the first time in twenty years he was again savoring genuine Ceylon tea. He thought about all he had had to forgo, and he thought about his late wife, how happy she would have been to see him step into the room with his head held high. "Here you are, my gazelle, genuine Ceylon tea, and . . ." Oh, the things he would have bought for her! Blue velvet for a dress she had yearned for her whole life. Yes, and henna for her hands—he wouldn't forget that. Year after year he had undertaken his trek to the officials but had come home empty-handed every time. His wife, however, had always encouraged him to ask the bishop, or else the son-in-law of the labor minister's chauffeur, for just one more letter of recommendation. She swore that when he did receive his pension she would color her hands with henna and jump for joy like a young bride and dance three times around the courtyard. Salim smiled bitterly.

In the distance someone had turned up the radio very loud. Salim knew for certain it was Mahmoud the butcher, a bachelor who, night after night, listened to the songs of the Egyptian singer Um Khulthum. Every Thursday night, Radio Cairo broadcast Um Khulthum into the wee hours. The butcher was enamored of her voice. He would often cry and dance around his little room, his only partner a pillow pressed inside his arms. And he wasn't the only one who idolized her. Millions of Arabs loved her so much that no head of state who took himself seriously dared give a speech on a Thursday evening—not one single Arab would have listened.

Like a wave, the singer's voice surged out of the room and across the small courtyard of the neighboring building, over to the dovecote, past the walkway crowded with flowers and climbing plants, and finally broke upon the wall. The sound cascaded into Salim's own courtyard and kept its course unerringly through the flood of other voices until it streamed into his ear.

Salim had always been a good listener, but silence simply didn't suit him. Only now, in the stillness of his soul, did he first discover that every voice has its own peculiar taste. His ear became a magical palate. He flitted from one voice to another like a butterfly. Um Khulthum's song had the beauty of a patch of carnations so carefully tended that not a single thistle strayed inside.

Salim tarried for a while in the singer's well-kept garden, then he was drawn away by the homelier blossoms of other voices. A sudden disturbance turned him toward a painful whispering that tasted a little overspiced. Salim smiled: Afifa was exaggerating again, she had a habit of making every burp or broken wind into an almost incurable disease. She would speak very softly, to cajole her listeners into believing that what she was saying was a matter of national security.

Suddenly he heard the concerned voice of an old woman. "God protect us all if it's true what they're saying about a cholera epidemic in the north." Salim froze. Cholera? So it was true! He had heard the news for the first time that very day on the BBC, but the state news agency had denied all reports: *"All rumors of a cholera epidemic are completely unfounded! Whoever says there is one is a foreign agent."*

"Who told you that?" Afifa wanted to get to what mattered most with cholera epidemics.

"I don't know, I just heard that the hospitals in Aleppo are full," answered the old woman, and Salim recognized her concern despite her lie. He was certain that she knew her source exactly, but there were several unknown guests playing backgammon with their neighbor Tanius, and two strangers had joined the card game at neighbor Elias's. That was reason enough to be cautious about every utterance. People said that the only thing to come out of the union with Nasser's Egypt was a new and improved secret police. No longer known by the modest name "Secret Service," it was now called the "National Security Service." Its nets were being woven even tighter, so tight that fathers and mothers were no longer sure of their own children, and neighbors lived in mutual distrust.

Salim tried to picture the expression on a speaker's face by the taste of his voice. Now and then he would stand up and look across the courtyard to check his accuracy, but his shortsighted eyes were no match for his sensitive ears. A blur of figures was all he could see.

The excited voice of one of the card players, who was threatening to throw down his cards and go home, tasted a little sour. The other players tried to calm the man down and assured him that no one had so much as glanced at his hand. Afifa and her guests were also whispering their concern, since the man was known for his temper. But the more the other players tried to pacify the man, the angrier he became. Finally one of the men he was accusing took up the threat, threw down his own cards, and said in a voice that was quiet but tasted of fire: "Go on! Leave! You're a miserable loser, anyway. We're just trying to have some fun, understand?" Each word, quiet as it was, bored into the ears like a flaming arrow. The player who had started the row in the first place immediately whimpered an apology. Salim smiled with satisfaction.

Salim stayed up the entire night, sitting on his sofa, even after all the neighbors' guests had gone home.

The last sounds he registered in the early morning

hours before he turned on his side and fell asleep were the loud chirping from under the pomegranate tree and some tender whispers from Afifa's bedroom.

Tuma the emigrant was the first to appear early that afternoon. He paced up and down Salim's room, asking where the others were keeping themselves so long. Then he sat down a while, stood up impatiently, and again started pacing quickly back and forth. It was eight o'clock before everyone arrived.

"It's been forever," the emigrant began, "since old Salim took his last trip. And that's exactly what's keeping him from speaking—the longing in his soul for foreign places." Tuma stopped, took a deep pull on the waterpipe, and passed it along.

"Okay"—Tuma's speech was infected with American idioms from his days in the United States—"we all know he's a born coachman! And what coachman ever rests once he's reached his destination, even if he's managed to find the most beautiful oasis in the world? Well? No coachman worth his whip. And that's what's made our friend sick."

At these words Salim nodded thoughtfully.

"He has to travel over seven mountains, through seven valleys, and across seven plains. He has to sleep under seven foreign skies in seven foreign cities, and you'll see, then his words will come back."

This idea so enthused the former minister that he

offered to cover all expenses. And Mehdi and Tuma offered to serve as travel guides.

The friends scoured Damascus for days until they secured an old coach. Their hopes rose when they saw Salim, with gleaming eyes and fresh attire, climb aboard and give his whip a masterful crack. Only bad coachmen actually hit their horses—the good ones only hint at what the horses will be spared if they obey. The horses trotted off, and a few neighbors cried as they waved goodbye.

Salim drove with his entourage through seven cities and over seven mountains. He crossed seven plains and valleys. The trip lasted forty days. He came back exhausted and excited, but still unable to speak. Tuma had to listen to the others complain about how much valuable time had been lost due to his suggestion.

Next came the nature healers—all kinds—and even Um Khalil, an experienced midwife. They administered to the coachman the most repugnant potions, ointments, and herbal concoctions imaginable, and Salim grew paler from day to day, but he was still unable to speak. Roman Catholic holy water was as ineffective as its Greek Orthodox competitor, and holy sand from Mecca did as little to free his tongue as dust from Bethlehem.

"There are only eight days left," said the former minister, full of worry, and his words terrified the entire group on that late night. They sat mutely in their circle, as if their fairies, too, had tied their tongues. The clock struck twelve, but despite the late hour the friends were not the least bit tired. "I've got it," the teacher cried out and slapped himself hard on the knee. "I know it for sure. It's as plain as day," he spoke loudly, as if he were trying to buck himself up after all the defeats. "It's seven stories—old Salim has to hear seven stories in order to regain his voice."

Musa the barber was immediately enthusiastic, but not the taciturn Ali. Tuma and Isam failed to find much merit in the proposal, whereas Junis was quickly convinced. Only the minister refrained from giving his opinion right away.

"Talk, talk, talk. That's all teachers and barbers know how to do! That's how you make your living," Isam waxed indignant.

"I don't have the faintest idea how to tell a story, and I don't think this rubbish is going to cure Salim," declared Ali.

The friends quarreled a long time, and it was almost dawn before the minister, full of concern for the old coachman's voice, was able to intervene. With well-chosen words he quieted the emigrant and Isam. Even Ali, himself at a loss for any other solution, agreed. "Go ahead," he said. "If that's what poor Salim wants, I won't stand in the way." And that was what Salim wanted.

"Who should start?" asked the barber, and the newly reconciled friends were once again quarreling. No one wanted to go first.

"Fine!" Isam shouted. "In prison, whenever we faced an unpleasant task, we would let the cards decide." He looked at Salim. "Do you have any playing cards?" Salim nodded, then stood up and fetched his old, crumpled deck of cards.

"Now watch!" Isam spoke quietly. "I am holding six cards. I put in one ace and shuffle them up. Whoever draws the ace tells the first story. Agreed?"

They all nodded their heads in silence. Only the barber spoke, to urge Isam to shuffle the cards well.

Isam lay the cards down on the small table. Because he was the oldest, the emigrant was allowed to draw first. He drew a jack, the café owner a deuce, and the barber a king. The teacher then pulled his card and flipped it over. It was the ace of spades. The former inmate, the minister, and the locksmith all sighed with relief.

Salim, however, was doubled over in silent laughter,
so that the barber once again began
to doubt whether the old coachman was really mute or simply
pulling their
leg.

5

Why
one man allowed
his voice to be chained,
and how he later set it free

Mehdi, a tall, haggard man, had taught geography for
thirty-five years. He couldn't put an exact number on
how many pupils he had acquainted with the countries of the world, their rivers and mountains, but he
was proud of counting among his former students
two bank directors, one general, and several doctors.
In the old quarter he commanded a certain respect—
which he basked in somewhat proudly—with the
result that many people respectfully avoided him. It
was difficult to converse with him at any length, at
least as an equal partner. Moreover, even if the talk
started with the weather, the latest price hikes, or a
cholera epidemic, sooner or later it always came back
to geography—and the ignorance of his interlocutor.
"If you don't know how high the Himalayas are, how
can you appreciate how low things really are here in
Damascus?" he is supposed to have said to a neighbor
with deliberate ambiguity. The gossipmongers on his
street dubbed him "Mister Himalaya" from that day
on. The only time Mehdi left geography out of the

conversation was when he met with Salim and his circle of friends.

That November afternoon dark clouds had once again gathered above Damascus. It had just rained for half an hour and the streets and people smelled of fresh earth. The air was cold as ice. Mehdi adjusted his scarf as he stepped outside. He greeted the Armenian cobbler sitting at his large sewing machine. The man peered over the rim of his lowered glasses and held up two fingers, to inform Mehdi that the new shoes the teacher was having made would be ready in two days.

"That's fine," Mehdi whispered and went his way. "When was the last time the cobbler actually smiled," he asked himself, but didn't know the answer.

A column of military vehicles rolled across the square in front of the Bab Tuma, or Thomas's Gate, and veered off to the east. The children were delighted by the spraying and splashing from the abundant puddles. "Charge! Off to the war!" they shouted with glee to the soldiers sitting crammed inside the trucks, who simply stared directly ahead, full of worry, completely oblivious to the general jubilation.

That spring, an uprising had broken out just across the border, in the Iraqi city of Mosul, and had ended in great bloodshed. The Iraqi regime accused Nasser of having financed and incited the rebels.

Something between the two countries had gone wrong. The Iraqi president Kassem, whom Radio

Damascus had proclaimed the hero of the Iraqi revolution only a year before, suddenly fell into disgrace, without the slightest explanation. From then on, the Syrian radio characterized him as the bloodthirsty "Butcher of Baghdad." Reports of starvation, rebellion, and cholera in Iraq were now filling the airwaves almost daily, but no mention was made of any unrest or open conflict in Syria itself. Rumor had it that a group of young Syrian officers had mutinied against the government. They were said to have captured important positions in the east with the help of Iraqi troops. Radio Damascus issued assurances that the situation in the east was calm, but Mehdi refused to believe the speaker's reassuring words. Governments in Syria, without exception, made a habit of proclaiming peace and order just when they were on the verge of collapse. A bitter feeling arose in Mehdi. What kind of times are these? The regime declares the dictator in a neighboring country a brother and a hero, then condemns him as an enemy and cowardly traitor, without asking the people of either nation for their opinion, although it was their sons who would be fighting each other if it came to war.

Mehdi glanced at the rifles. Like the faces of the young soldiers, they were shiny and clean on the outside, but on the inside, charged and loaded.

That day, he had left his house, located near the French hospital, a little earlier than usual. He was overcome with a longing to see his childhood home on Bakri Street. It wouldn't take him very far out of the way. When Mehdi spotted the house, in which he had not set foot for over forty years, he was surprised at how tiny the door actually was; it had seemed like such a mighty gate when he was a child. His heart started pounding. As is often the case in Damascus, the front door was slightly ajar. He pushed it open. The smell of laundry and heating oil immediately came to greet him from the courtyard.

A small barefoot girl ran up to him. Mehdi smiled at her. "What's your name, little girl?"

"Ibtisam," the girl answered. Mehdi heard the clatter of wooden house shoes. An ample woman came out of the room that had once served his parents as a bedroom. When she saw Mehdi, she smiled, though slightly flustered. "That's the third time today she's gotten away from me! God is my witness, the devil himself would sooner fast and pray and make a pilgrimage than attempt to give these children a bath. Six of them, and each one like quicksilver! You just keep grabbing at nothing!" The woman paused and grabbed her daughter by the shoulder. "But come in! May I get something for you?" she invited Mehdi inside.

"No, thank you, I only wanted to have a look. You see, I was born in this house. We used to live here a long time ago. My grandparents, too. Mohammed

Riad al-Karim—his name is chiseled in the marble plate above the door. That was my grandfather," Mehdi said, a little embarrassed.

"You don't say! And could you get water on the third floor in those days?" Without waiting for his answer, the woman continued: "For a year now the pressure's been so low it only flows down here. The neighbors from upstairs have to fetch their water from us, and every Saturday, when it's bath day, there's always a big fracas."

"No, back then there was enough water. How many families are living here now, anyway?"

"Three upstairs and two downstairs, plus one student, but he doesn't need much water. He always takes his wash home on the weekend. He's from Daraia. A very courteous man. Our little Ibtisam likes to sleep in his bed most of all. He really loves the children. But I keep telling them to leave the man in peace. You ought to see the thick books he plows through night after night!" The woman illustrated her speech with her hands.

Mehdi looked at the small room next to the staircase. "And who lives there?"

"In that little-bitty room? My dear man, God have mercy on your eyes! You think a human being could live in there? That room barely holds three oil heaters in the summer and two bicycles in the winter. Take another look!"

Mehdi was visibly shocked when he peered into

the tiny room. He said goodbye quietly and left. And although his wife had asked him to buy fish for the next day at Batbuta's—right near Bakri Street—he forgot all about it. Batbuta the fishmonger was shouting so loud they could hear him in Turkey, but Mehdi walked quickly past his shop. Not even the pungent smell of fish could jolt him from his thoughts.

All six friends had already gathered at Salim's by the time Mehdi opened the door to the coachman's room. No one ever had to knock. Isam was kneeling in the corner in front of the wood stove, puffing away. The room smelled pleasant, like burnt resin. Mehdi closed the door behind him, just as Isam exclaimed, "Finally!" A little flame was glowing inside the pile of wood.

"I've run out of breath. I used to be able to blow a fire hot enough to roast a whole mutton to a crisp," Isam sighed and coughed.

"Good evening!" Mehdi greeted everyone and rubbed his hands; he was delighted by the tea's aroma.

The minister was the first to notice that Mehdi was wearing his brown suit, along with a white shirt and a brownish scarf made of silk.

"Have you been to a wedding?" he teased him, then stood up like the others and shook hands with his friend.

"All right, I'm going to start," Mehdi said after a short while and took a hefty swallow of tea, as if he wanted to prepare his vocal cords for the great task that lay ahead. "Now open your ears and your hearts. May God grant you health and a long life if you pay close attention to what I say," the teacher began.

"Just a moment, please," begged Tuma the emigrant as he took his glasses out of their leather case and put them on. The others grinned, because Tuma always insisted on wearing his glasses whenever he listened to their stories. "Okay, now I can pay close attention to what you're going to say," Tuma added, smiling contentedly.

"I'll never understand that," said Mehdi. "Old Socrates used to say, if one of his pupils was sitting without saying a word, 'Speak so that I may see you,' whereas you—you want to hear me with your eyes?"

"That's right, man," groaned Tuma.

"All right, but before I begin, I wish to confess to you, my dear friends, the reason why I like telling stories. I like to tell them because one story I heard as a child completely enthralled me. First let me tell you how I came upon this strange tale.

"I was a small child when my father, blessed may he rest in God's bosom, brought home a new apprentice. My father was a carpenter, and his new helper came from a faraway village. He was poor and had nowhere to stay in Damascus, so we cleaned out a little room by the stairs, and Shafak, as he was called, started living in this tiny room. The space seemed fairly large to me when I was a child, but in reality it's so small it can't even hold three oil heaters. In any case, I can still see his face exactly—it was completely covered with scars—although I can't remember how old he was. When he came home in the evening he would wash himself, eat, drink his tea and sit on a small chair in front of his room, smoke, and gaze up at the sky. He would sit there for hours without moving a muscle, just staring at the stars. Whenever the sky stayed overcast for more than a day, which rarely happened in winter, I would notice how uneasy he became. He would withdraw into his room, but stay awake long into the night. Since my room was opposite his, on the other side of the courtyard, I could see his room from my bed. I watched him every night. His room didn't have any electricity, so he always left the oil lamp on for a long time. Sometimes he would pace up and down. Whenever I woke up in the middle of the night to go to the toilet, he was always still awake, even though he had to get up early every day. My father, on the other hand, never once in his life managed to keep his eyes open after ten o'clock.

"All right, so my father liked him very much—mostly because he secured a huge commission the day Shafak started. 'I owe that to Shafak,' he said, 'his face is truly blessed.' He repeated that very phrase for years, whenever Shafak's name came up in conversation.

"Shafak was very shy and always spoke in a quiet

tone of voice. Whenever my mother or my sister talked to him he would look down at the floor in embarrassment. The children from the courtyard made fun of his shyness, and had they not been afraid of my father, they would have pelted him with stones. My father, however, loved Shafak as if he were his own son.

"All right, to make a long story short, I was completely convinced that Shafak was a magician. And although I was curious even as a child, I never entered his room. I was a little afraid of him. In fact, my aunt made my mother secretly promise to keep him away from us children. 'Have you seen his eyes? They don't have any color. And his teeth? Have you seen his teeth, the way they're set in two rows? Two on top and two underneath,' my aunt muttered, full of fear.

" 'Yes, yes,' my mother laughed, 'and I've seen his toes, too. They're webbed just like a duck's.'

"My aunt became annoyed, and I became really afraid of Shafak.

"One summer day he was sitting on his small chair as usual, watching the heavens. I went over to him and asked him what he was looking for.

" 'Two stars who love each other. One of them sparkles like a diamond and the other is fire-red. They're chasing each other. Sometimes the diamond is in the lead, sometimes the other one. If they ever come together, then a thousand and one pearls will drop from the sky. And all the oysters in the seas will open their mouths to receive their pearls. And if a human being witnesses this moment and holds out his palm, then he'll receive a pearl as well. But he's not allowed to keep it, he has to dance in a circle three times, with his hand held open, and fling the pearl into the sky—and then he'll be happy for the rest of his life.'

" 'But why are the stars chasing each other in the first place?' I asked.

" 'That's a long story,' replied the carpenter's helper. 'But how can I tell it to you? I'll miss the moment when it happens! Still, if you promise to watch the sky while I tell you about this amazing love, and promise to yell as soon as you see the two stars come together, so that I can hold out my palm, then I will tell you the story of the stars.'

"I promised Shafak I would watch the stars, and this is the story he told me:

"It all happened in days that have long since disappeared. There was a farmer who had a magical voice. Whenever he sang, people would cry and laugh, and whenever he told stories, people would listen intently and forget all their worries and cares. But not only was he famous for his voice; his hands, too, could paint winds, caravans, and roses so clearly that people could see, smell, and taste his words.

"The farmer was as poor as a beggar; nevertheless, with his voice he succeeded in charming the most beautiful woman in the village. Sahar, as she was called, fell in love with him at first sight and cast to the wind all the entreaties of the rich farmers who were courting her. One wealthy but aged merchant offered her parents their daughter's weight in gold, but she refused him, too. 'I'd rather eat dry bread and olives and listen to my poor farmer's voice than stuff myself full of the merchant's roasted gazelle and have him ruin my day with his roaring and my night with his snoring.' Her kind parents gave Sahar their blessing and soon celebrated the wedding of their daughter with her beloved. Not every daughter is granted such good fortune.

"The farmer took tremendous pains to improve his poor state, but he was born jinxed. Whatever he undertook failed. If his fingers touched gold, the noble metal turned to hay. May God protect you from such bad fortune! But people still envied him his voice.

" 'For your voice,' the village elder once told him, 'I would gladly trade you all my fields.'

"Another farmer exclaimed, 'If God would give me just one tiny bit of your magical windpipe instead of my rasping voice, I swear, I would give you my whole flock.'

"All right, so the years passed, and every year this farmer became poorer and poorer, until one summer, when his wheat fell victim to a blight, he cursed heaven. Poverty had eaten him out of house and home. His debts were so great that he had to sell off his wardrobe and his bed. 'The wardrobe was always empty anyway,' he consoled his wife, 'and we can sleep on the floor just as well!'

"But he couldn't live two weeks off the money brought by the sale. The entire district spoke of his bad luck, and even though he could sing and tell stories so beautifully, no one wanted to invite him to weddings, as they had in the past. They were afraid that with his wretched luck he might bring the newlyweds misfortune.

"His wife, Sahar, was teased whenever she went to the village well to fetch water. 'Does his voice keep you warm in winter? When you get hungry, do you boil his voice or do you roast it?' the women called after her. Sahar wept bitterly, but once home she would laugh and try to cheer her husband. Nonetheless he sensed her sadness, and it cut deeply into his heart.

"One day, although it was icy-cold outside, the farmer tried to sell his old jacket, in order to purchase some millet for himself and his wife. But no one wanted to buy it. The farmer was ashamed to return home empty-handed. He ran into the nearby forest and from the depths of his soul screamed out his pain. 'I've been as patient as a camel!' he cried. 'I've prayed to all the good angels for help, but their hearts have been cold and all they've done is stop their ears. Tell me, you demons of evil, what else do you desire of me?'

" 'Your voice!' The words echoed in the woods. An icy chill ran through his body and the farmer shivered and shook. He turned around and saw a man in a glistening dark mantle who said, 'I will pay you an inexhaustible supply of money to buy your voice!'

" 'I'll give it to you if you'll just keep my wife and me fed for a week. My voice, my voice, no one has wanted to listen to me for over a year, anyway,' the farmer moaned.

" 'You misunderstand me. I want to buy *all* your speech, not just your beautiful voice. Neither your hands nor your eyes will be able to speak. But in return you will receive this gold lira, which you will never be able to use up. Whenever it leaves your hand, it will give birth to another. As long as you live, you will never be able to spend it,' said the man, and his eyes burned like two glowing stones.

" 'That sounds fair enough!' the farmer cried out. The man walked toward him, and in a flash he threw his cape around the poor farmer, and swept him away into a whirlpool of darkness. The cape weighed on the farmer's shoulders more and more heavily, until his knees buckled under its weight. He groped about, searching for something to cling to, but his hands slid off the wizard—for that's what he was—as if he were a cold column of marble. There was a great stench of decay. The farmer had to cough, his throat hurt as if he had swallowed a knife. Then he fell to the ground, unconscious.

"When he came to he was lying on the cold forest ground. A gold lira was glimmering in his hand. He hurried home. His wife was filled with worry when she saw his pale face. 'What's wrong, my love?'

"Exhausted, the farmer sat down on the mattress and held out his hand to give her the gold lira. Beaming with joy, his wife took the coin and hurried away. But before she had left the room, the farmer again felt the coldness of metal in his clenched fist. He opened it, and there he saw a second gold lira.

"Meanwhile, his elated wife hurried to the butcher, the vegetable peddler, and the baker, yet the prices for all the things she bought amounted to only a few pieces of silver. Holding her head high, she placed an order with the carpenter for his most expensive bed—made of prized oak. She also purchased a new, warm jacket for her husband and a colorful dress she had long desired. The village boys carried her full baskets home, and they were grateful to her for the few piasters she gave them. The farmer's wife bought all of that for just one gold lira. At that time you could buy a house for five gold liras.

"News of the gold lira spread through the village like wildfire. Some people figured the farmer had used his voice to charm a fairy, who had presented him with a hidden treasure. Others guessed he had robbed a traveler. But no one had any idea, not even the farmer himself, how dearly he had paid for his treasure.

"All right, so when Sahar came back, she noticed that her husband was not only unable to speak, he was also incapable of making the slightest gesture. He couldn't even express a tiny bit of joy at all the delicacies she had brought home. He chewed his food in silence and stared off into space with dead eyes.

"The next morning, the farmer again stretched out his hand with the gold lira. That was all he could do. His wife sat across from him, staring wide-eyed at his hand. As soon as she took the coin from his palm and placed it on the table, a second one took its place. The farmer took hundreds of gold liras from his hand. But he couldn't even smile, for smiling is also a language, and what a heavenly language it is! And his flute, from which he had once coaxed the most magical melodies, would not produce a single note.

"The man took a piece of paper to draw his wife a picture explaining what had happened, but his hand was no longer subject to his will. All he could produce were meaningless zigzags, but clever Sahar saw in those lines the face of the devil.

" 'Don't worry, my heart,' his good wife consoled him, 'I will be your tongue. I will heal you, even if I have to run every last healer on the planet through a sieve to find the very best.'

"Sahar used the money to build a dream palace. A host of servants, jesters, and musicians were retained to see to her husband's happiness. Her stables housed only the noblest horses of the Arabian desert. And if angels had flown above her garden instead of swallows, people would have thought it the Garden of Eden."

"I actually prefer swallows," Isam interrupted and then laughed at his own thought. "Just imagine, angels whizzing around six feet above your head. You couldn't even enjoy your waterpipe, they'd be flying so low." He puffed out a small cloud of smoke. "Have you heard the joke about the devout man who felt some birdshit hit his head and thanked the Lord for not equipping cows with wings?"

"Quiet!" the barber hissed and turned back to Mehdi. "Please, go on."

"All right, so the woman built a paradise for her husband with her love and the inexhaustible supply of gold, but all he could do was walk around joylessly, his face pale, as if he were in another world.

"The woman's emissaries searched the world over for medicine men and wise women who could heal her husband. Sahar promised their weight in gold if they could restore her husband's voice. True healers and charlatans came in droves, ate their fill, and traveled on. But the farmer remained mute. His rooms were filled to the ceiling with gold, but in his heart he felt poorer than a mangy dog. He couldn't speak a word, nothing, not with his eyes, not with his hands.

"One day Sahar woke up and looked for her husband—in vain. He had disappeared. A servant reported seeing his master ride away on his stallion.

"Sahar had the entire district searched high and low for him, but the servants came back at sunset every day for seven days and shook their heads. Still, Sahar didn't give up, and whenever an explorer brought news of a rider on a stallion along the banks of the Euphrates or the Nile, she would send messengers bearing her request to the local rulers, and these in turn would send search parties throughout the region. No stone was left unturned, for Sahar promised a marble palace to the warden, mayor, steward, or prince, whichever happy soul would find her husband. In vain.

"The farmer, meanwhile, scoured the earth for the wizard who had bought his voice. He chased after every clue faster than the wind, but the wizard was nowhere to be found. Wherever people had suddenly lost their voices, the wizard had come and gone, leaving behind nothing but another breathing corpse, incapable of expressing sadness or joy, pain or happiness.

"One day—his search was now in its third year, and he was ready to give up—the exhausted farmer was resting at a village fair, listening to a man singing in a wonderful voice. Just as the singer was about to finish, a young merchant wearing a broad cape asked him to repeat the last love song, and threw him a gold coin. The singer took a bow and sang the song even more movingly. The farmer was sitting close to the stage. Now, just before the song was over, the merchant walked over to the singer, whispered something in his ear, and moved back into the shadows of the stage. As he passed by the farmer, a cloud of rose perfume filled the air, but the farmer smelled the stench of decay beneath the sweet cloak of roses. His blood froze in his veins. It was the same smell that had filled his lungs before he had lost consciousness, a smell he would never forget as long as he lived. He tiptoed backstage and watched the merchant.

"All right, so in less than a quarter-hour the singer left the stage. The merchant spoke to the singer for a while, then threw his cape over the poor man. The farmer stared as the singer's body shook and quickly sank to the ground, lifeless. But what happened next was unbelievable. The wizard flung back his cape and behold, beside him stood the spitting image of the singer, and both walked away together, talking as if they were friends.

"The farmer was now certain he had found the wizard and ran after him in pursuit. He chased him for two days and two nights. The wizard and his companion seemed never to tire; and when the third day dawned, they kept going as spryly as they had on the first. In order not to fall asleep, the farmer cut his hand and rubbed salt in the wound. The pain made it possible for him to stay awake through the third day. At dawn on the fourth day, he saw a castle rising slowly from the mist in the valley. The farmer was spellbound. As he marveled at the wondrous sight, he forgot about the salt and soon fell asleep. How long he slept he didn't know: perhaps just for a moment, perhaps for several days. A thunderclap startled him awake, and he leapt to his feet. Standing before him he saw the wizard, tall and mighty as a palm tree. 'Why are you following me?' he roared. The man was unable to answer. He couldn't even nod. 'You have been richly rewarded. There is no going back!' the wizard cried. The farmer hurled himself upon him, but the wizard tossed him aside in a high arc and hurried off. When the man stood up, he saw the distant castle disappearing slowly in the fog.

"For years the farmer followed the wizard, but time and again he simply dropped from sight. Nonetheless the farmer refused to give up.

"One spring day he was taking a brief rest by a pond and thinking how he could outsmart the wizard when he spotted a young woman drawing water with a sieve. She managed to run a few steps before the water drained completely, then turned around in despair and went back to the pond, where she started all over again. The woman looked tired, but she didn't give up. 'I must complete the task. I absolutely have to, even if it costs me my life. I have to finish.' The woman spoke out loud to lift her spirits, crying bitterly all the while.

"The farmer grabbed the woman by the arm.

" 'Let go of me, I have to fill this sieve with water and take it to the king of the demons so he will release my husband,' the woman said and tore herself from the farmer's grasp. Again she scooped some water, but in a trice it vanished through the sieve.

"The farmer grabbed her once more and gently took the sieve from her hand. The woman shouted and beat the farmer until she was so exhausted all she could do was curse him feebly. He, however, walked slowly to a nearby grotto that the farmers filled with snow in the winter so that the rock cistern inside would have water for the summer. The grotto was packed to the brim with snow. He scooped a large amount into the sieve and hurried back to the woman, who was standing by the pond, sobbing in despair. The moment she saw the sieve filled with snow she beamed. She jumped up, took it in her hands, and flew hurriedly away, for she was a demoness herself—may God protect you from her wrath!

"All right, so after a short while the woman came back with her beloved. They thanked the farmer, and when they saw that neither his eyes nor his hands could speak, they knew that he had sold his voice to the wizard.

" 'You are the only one who can free your voice,' the demon said softly. 'He locks the voices up in his castle and uses them to create his elixir. No demon on earth can gain entrance to his castle, but with my help you will be able to. I shall change you into an eagle and you can search earth, heaven, and hell for the castle. When you find it, do not look back. Whatever you hear, do not look back. For if you do, the castle will be gone forever. Find the blue window that looks to heaven and dive right into it. The moment you break through that window you will turn back into a man. If you leave through the same window, you'll turn once more into an eagle. Take a sliver of the broken glass and hide it under your tongue, for as long as you keep this sliver, the castle cannot escape you. Look for your voice inside the castle—it will be your own image. Hug it close to you; that way you will set it free. But do not forget the glass sliver even for a second. The wizard will attempt to repair the broken windowpane in order to hide his castle in the fog of eternity, but as long as the smallest piece is missing, he will be unable to protect the castle against the might of Time. After seven nights it will collapse. Then the voices will lose their chains, but they will wander the earth until the end of time if they cannot be united with their images. Do not forget the splinter! The wizard will do everything he can to save his castle.'

"All right, so the demon kissed the man between his eyes and sent him soaring into heaven as an eagle. The demon and his wife watched the king of birds disappear into the blue sky. The demoness was still lost in thought when her beloved took her in his arms and kissed her on the lips. Two corn-poppy blossoms sprang from the spot where her feet had touched the earth.

"For years the eagle combed earth, heaven, and hell for the wizard's castle. During this time his wife searched desperately for him. Just as she was about to give up all hope, there suddenly appeared in her courtyard an old man with a long beard as white as snow. The horses shied and the dogs whimpered as if they felt an earthquake coming.

" 'Would you like your husband back? In return I wish neither castles nor gold,' said the old man, who then ran his fingers thoughtfully through his beard and peered at Sahar with eyes as red as fire.

" 'Of course I want my husband back, but what is your price if you want neither gold nor castles?'

" 'Your voice,' the old man said quietly. 'Give me your voice and in seven nights you will be lying in his arms.'

" 'I will never sell my voice! Be gone!' Sahar shouted, although her heart burned with longing for her husband.

" 'I will be back,' the wizard replied and walked slowly out of the courtyard.

"Three months later the old man returned, but Sahar again sent him away, with a heavy heart.

" 'The third time I come back will be the last. Consider my offer carefully!' the old man said angrily and slammed the door behind him.

"Sahar waited and waited, but it was three years before the old man returned. 'Well, have you considered my offer, carefully?' he asked, and a smile played around his lips.

" 'Take it. I want him.' Sahar said quietly.

"The wizard threw his cape over her, and when she came to, she could no longer speak. The servants were frightened when they saw their mistress coming out of her chamber looking so pale, for only a little while before they had watched her slowly leave the castle with the old man and climb aboard his carriage.

"Meanwhile, the eagle searched and searched. He circled above all the valleys and mountains of earth, heaven, and hell. One day, as he was circling over the earth, he saw a castle rising from the depths of a valley. Shortly thereafter he recognized the wizard hurrying into the castle with a woman. He wanted most of all to pluck out the wizard's eyes, but he knew that the castle would vanish on the spot. So he circled again and saw a golden dome with four windows: one red, one green, one blue, and one black. God only knows what the other three windows were for," said Mehdi, who then took a few draws on the waterpipe and passed it to Junis.

"Blue for heaven, red for sin, black for . . ." Isam tried to explain.

"You heard him," replied Musa, "he said God only knows what they were for. Are you God now, or

what? Please, go on, don't leave out a single word,"
he begged Mehdi.

"All right, so after searching for a long time the
eagle found the blue window that looked to heaven,
but at the same moment he heard his wife crying for
help behind him. He wanted to turn around, but he
remembered the kind demon's warning. Straight as
an arrow he flew into the window with all his might.
The glass shattered. The eagle took a sliver in his beak
and jumped through. And then it happened exactly as
the demon had promised: he was once again a human
being. Now he tore off part of his shirt, wrapped up
the sharp sliver and shoved it under his tongue.

"Two rows of rooms lined an endless hall. The
farmer pricked up his ears and soon made out a song
in a foreign language coming from the first room. He
carefully opened the door, and inside he saw over
forty young people, men and women, in foreign
dress. They were chained to the wall, but they
seemed refreshed and cheerful, as if they had just
arrived. They paid him no notice, as if they couldn't
see him. The farmer now hurried from door to door,
opening each one and looking for himself among the
many singers and storytellers. Then, outside the
thirty-third room, he heard his own voice. He
pushed open the door and saw his image chained to
the wall. With the strength of all his love for his own
voice he tore the chains off the wall and embraced his

image. 'Sahar!' he cried out loud, and his heart fluttered wildly with joy, like a bird just escaped from a cage.

"It wasn't long before he heard the wizard on the roof, bellowing furiously, for he was trying in vain to piece together the broken window. 'I smell a human,' the voice of the wizard echoed through the halls of the castle. For a moment the farmer was crippled with fear, but he ran as fast as he could and leaped back through the window into the open sky. A great eagle with mighty wings climbed the heavens. 'I'll get you!' cursed the wizard from the roof of his castle. He, too, changed into an eagle, but the farmer was faster. Then the wizard changed into a gusty wind and tried to knock the eagle down, but the eagle was stronger than the wind. He flew unerringly for two days and two nights. Hunger tore at his stomach. The wizard turned into a dove that fluttered helplessly in front of the eagle, but the eagle flew on. On the third day, the eagle was so thirsty he would have given everything in the world for a drop of water, but when he spotted a blue lake beyond the mountains he remembered the splinter underneath his tongue and was afraid. He flew on, and the lake dried up at once, for it had been none other than the wizard. Late in the afternoon of the third day, the eagle reached his palace. He flew through the open door of his bedroom, and there he saw Sahar lying on the bed. The moment he saw her dead eyes, the farmer knew that she had given up her voice for him. Sahar realized the eagle was her husband, because she recognized his eyes, the eyes that she had missed all those many years—but she couldn't speak a word to him.

" 'Come with me to rescue your voice!' the eagle said in the warm voice that Sahar had always loved. She climbed onto his back, and the eagle flew off.

"Now, the wizard knew the farmer would return. He went back to his castle and waited in front of Sahar's image. Day and night he waited, and late in the afternoon of the sixth day the farmer and his wife flew through the blue window that looked to heaven. Sahar wished for all the words in the world to tell her husband—who was now standing before her—how much she loved him, but she couldn't bring a single sound across her lips. Her husband whispered to her very softly: 'We have to find your image, and once you see it, do not look back, no matter how much I scream. Tear it from its chains and run out. Did you hear me? Save yourself!' He took Sahar in his arms. One final embrace, and then they tiptoed down the hall.

"When they heard Sahar's voice, they burst into the room. There stood the wizard. He was still tall and strong, but his face was pale, and his hair was streaked with gray. 'Give me the sliver and take your wife's image!' he said in a rattled voice.

" 'Never in my life!' the farmer answered and hurled himself upon the wizard, who at that very moment turned into a gigantic snake that wrapped itself around the image of Sahar. The farmer smote the reptile's head, and Sahar was able to free her voice from its chains. 'Go!' he cried as he struggled with the snake. He had almost strangled it when it turned into a scorpion that gave the farmer two venomous stings. The man cried out in pain and stomped on the scorpion, which instantly turned into a tiger, which fell upon the man. Sahar hadn't run more than two steps when she heard the thudding blows; she went back, took the chain that was lying on the floor and beat the tiger until it released her bleeding husband. The farmer looked at Sahar in astonishment and urgently waved her on, but she stood in front of her husband and kept striking away at the bleeding beast. Suddenly the tiger disappeared. The farmer felt death slowly creeping into his limbs. He drew Sahar to him and kissed her on the lips. Carefully he passed into her mouth the glass sliver, still wrapped in its cloth.

"Sahar now knew that her beloved husband was fated to die. She cried out loud and clutched his head tightly to her breast. The wizard, who had changed himself into a gust of wind, noticed that the splinter was now in Sahar's mouth. But at the same time he also felt his end was nearing and turned himself into a poisonous spider. Suddenly Sahar felt a bite on her neck. She slapped herself with all her might. The spider dropped to the floor, dead.

"The two lovers died embracing each other. That same night a thousand and one voices slipped away from the ruins of the castle. Some of them found their images, and some are still looking to this very day. But at midnight on the dot two stars shot from the castle ruins up into the sky. One of them sparkled like a diamond, the other was fire-red.

"Ever since that day the red star has been following the sparkling Sahar star, and when they meet each other, a thousand and one pearls will fall into the open mouths of the oysters. And in that night the birds will sing marvelous songs late into the wee hours.

"That's what my father's helper told me," Mehdi said, "and when he had finished speaking, I asked with the curiosity of a child: 'And what's the name of the fire-red star?'

" 'Shafak,' he replied."

"May God bless your mouth for this story!" Faris was the first to speak. The others nodded their heads.

"But what happened to the apprentice?" asked the barber.

Mehdi paused for a long time. "You won't believe it. One night I heard a shout of joy. I woke up, pulled back the curtain and saw Shafak dancing in the court-yard. He was dancing with his hand outstretched, and a pearl was gleaming in his palm. He spun around one more time and flung the pearl into the sky. The next morning I told this to my mother. She just laughed at me and claimed I must have dreamt it—but Shafak disappeared that very day."

"Are you serious?" the minister made sure, and Mehdi nodded in silence. Only Salim gave an odd smile.

"If a fairy changed me into a star right now they'd call me the yawning star," Musa said, then yawned loudly and stood up. It was already after midnight.

"Before we go," Isam interjected without getting up, "we should draw cards to find out who's next."

"Oh, right, that's right," mumbled the locksmith like a child who has been caught in the act. Isam placed six cards on the table.

"I'd prefer to take the last card, you go ahead," Ali snapped at Tuma the emigrant, who was prodding him to draw. But it was the café owner, Junis, who drew the ace.

6

How
Salim without
saying a word talked a
merchant into lowering his price

Salim hadn't spent such a peaceful night in a long time. Sleep drove the fatigue of the last months out of his bones. When he woke up, he saw Afifa standing right outside his window, despite the icy cold. She gave an embarrassed smile. "May today bring good fortune to you, Uncle! Will you join us for some coffee?" she called to him. The old coachman shook his head with a smile and jumped merrily out of his bed.

Shortly after eight the baker's boy brought him his bread. Ever since he had received his pension, Salim had been giving the lad a piaster every morning.

That morning the olives tasted especially delicious with the warm pita bread and hot tea. Salim started thinking about the teacher's story, and about Sahar and Shafak. What ever became of the carpenter's apprentice? Was he really the fire-red star, or just a storytelling carpenter? With these questions in his head he cleared his little table, locked the door to his room, stored the key inside his leather bag, and hurried out of the house.

At that hour his street was still quiet: the children had long since gone to school. In the summer, the cries of one vegetable peddler overlap with those of the next, but on this wintry day only a single man could be seen slowly pushing his cart past the houses. And all he was hawking in the courtyards was a couple of onions and a pitiful pile of potatoes. "Seven pounds for one lira!" His whiny voice was practically begging. The dog that belonged to the pastry chef Nassif was barking incessantly as it did every day. A small mongrel with a big mouth, it began yapping when the sun rose and continued throughout the day until its master, a wealthy widower, came home. Many housewives were on the verge of despair. And the barking was also a constant annoyance to the men of the neighborhood. One day Afifa's oldest son, goaded on by his mother, climbed the wall, stuffed the dog into a sack, and let it loose in a field on the outskirts of the city. But the cur found its way back to its owner. Until then, the neighborhood believed that only cats come back. A dog, they imagined, would wag its tail and follow anyone who tossed it a bone. But they had seen for themselves: this mongrel, half starved and wholly shaggy, leaping into the open arms of the teary-eyed pastry chef.

The saw that belonged to Ismat the carpenter broke the brief silence that had arisen between two barked chords—just as Salim was wondering about Afifa's watch at his window. What had she been

looking for? Was she spying on him to see whether he would talk in his sleep? He shook his head to free himself from his suspicion.

Every street has its own face, its own smell, and its own voice. Abara Street, where Salim lived, has an old, earth-colored face covered with furrows, children's scribblings, and stories. The windows wake up each morning bursting with curiosity as they wait for every bit of news, for every swift and swallow, for every scent. The street smells of anise even in winter: about halfway down the block there is an enormous anise warehouse belonging to two brothers. People tell the craziest stories about their miserliness. Apparently the two brothers fell in love at the same time, with two sisters—and were overjoyed they would only have to pay one priest at the wedding. It seems that everything was working out very well, until three months into their engagement, when one of the ladies suggested: "Every day you come and sit here until midnight. Why don't we hire a carriage, just for once, take a nice drive around Damascus, and then have some ice cream at Bekdash's in the Hamadiya bazaar." The brothers gazed at one another in horror, rose from their seats, and slowly staggered out on wobbly legs. They spent the rest of their lives celebrating their last-minute escape from the two spendthrifts, and neither brother ever married. People told many stories about their stinginess, but neither their own millions nor their neighbors' disdain made a

whit of difference where that was concerned. On the contrary, the older and richer they grew, the more miserly they became.

On this particular morning the younger brother appeared on the balcony and shouted down to the potato peddler: "Are those potatoes firm?" The vendor only turned around quickly and called back up with a bitter smile: "I'm not selling. I'm just out for a walk."

"Outrageous. These people whine about not having any business and then it turns out they're just out for a walk!" The millionaire waxed indignant.

"Once burned, twice shy," thought Salim, and he, too, smiled bitterly. Indeed, the peddler knew the brothers all too well. Only a newcomer would have been taken in by that polite question. The minute he pushed his cart up to their door, both brothers would throw themselves on his wares, and an hour later the peddler would be exhausted and all his vegetables nibbled and gnawed. The brothers' surefire methods guaranteed that both would come away from the transaction with full stomachs. First they would munch on something, then say in a horrified tone: "Now see here, do you think we're that dumb? You can't charge a whole lira for this half-eaten head of lettuce!" Nor were they above devouring unwashed cauliflower, lettuce leaves, or carrots.

The miserly brothers lived like recluses, as if they didn't belong to the neighborhood. An old man with

crooked legs sifted the anise for them through huge wire sieves from morning to night and packed it into large burlap sacks. Salim had known the man for over fifty years. He never spoke, but he showed up every morning and disappeared into the anise dust. Over time Salim noted that the man was shrinking. His legs became more crooked with every passing year, and his face took on the gray-green color of aniseed.

The Street Called Straight, which leads into Abara Street, has a different smell entirely. The musty odor of the pub hits you the moment you reach the crossing. The street itself reeks of horses and sweat, and were it not for Karim the fruit vendor the stench would be unbearable.

Karim sold what may have been the best fruit in the world. It always cost a little more than elsewhere, but it looked magnificent and gave off a wonderful bouquet. Fruit, you see, is first eaten with the eyes, then with the nose, and only lastly with the mouth. Karim did tend to exaggerate in praising his produce: "Whatever you can't smell from five yards away is yours for free!" But there was no question that the aromas wafted further than just around the corner. Karim lined the entrance to his shop with two rows of fruit crates; they looked like two rows of colorful teeth belonging to some gigantic mouth.

In fact, the whole street looked like a giant mouth lined with festive teeth made of packaged candies and nuts that glistened plump and tempting. No wonder

people were so eager to stick their heads inside the great gorge of the Street Called Straight. Just as rich old Damascenes decorate their mouths with gold teeth, so the venerable Damascus streets have adorned themselves since Roman times with carpets, nuts, copper kettles, and elaborately inlaid woodwork.

Salim shut his eyes and proceeded, very slowly, testing the street with his ears and his nose. Beyond the crossing he could make out the sweet voice of the drink vendor. "Come in, come in"—he encouraged every passerby to step inside. Salim wondered whether he could have ever guessed, judging by the high voice alone, that the man was as fat as he was. One step farther things came to a complete hush, and Salim took in an unusual smell. Yes, that was the apothecary. Salim smiled, and just then he heard Hassan the shoeshine man: "Shoeshine? *Happy Dew, here I am!* Shoe-shiiiine!"

Suddenly, with his eyes still closed, Salim saw Hassan the one-eyed farmer, who at the crack of dawn, every day for decades, had led his ten Damascus goats —this was an especially docile breed of goat, with soft, red hair and large, well-rounded udders— through the streets of the city selling the fresh, warm milk. A year before, the government had ordered him to stop, claiming that the milk was unhygienic and that the goats were an eyesore that marred the image of the city. The farmer, however, stubbornly per-

sisted in coming to town despite the police warnings —until his goats were finally confiscated.

So now, whenever there were funeral processions, Hassan would carry the floral wreaths in front of the coffins, or else he would help the flower seller Nuri with weddings, presenting magnificent bouquets to the celebrants. But when nobody was dying or getting married, Hassan would kill time by shining shoes. He was convinced that one day his goats would break out of their captivity and find him here, where he used to take a little rest each day, after covering three streets, to feed his beloved animals.

Whether Hassan was carrying bridal bouquets or polishing shoes, he always called out loudly to his goats. Only at funerals did he lower his voice and simply murmur their names quietly. People made fun of him, but Hassan was absolutely certain his ten goats would soon appear. He might occasionally forget to eat his lunch, but never, ever, had he confused one goat with another. "No, Happy Dew has a round white spot between her eyes but no black dot on her left ear like her twin sister, Cool Breeze," he would answer testily when people teased him by mixing up the names of his goats. "Shoe-shiiine, Salim, my friend? Greetings! *Silver Moon, here I am!* Shoe-shiiine!" he called out again loudly.

Salim touched the shoeshine man on the shoulder and steered around his pungent shoeshine box. One

step more and he could hear the noises of the wood-working shop, famous for its fine inlay. The old coachman, afraid he might at any moment trip over one of the wooden boxes drying in the winter sun, proceeded cautiously along his way. So he was all the more surprised when he stepped right into a deep, muddy pothole and lost his balance. Flinging his arms out wide, he hit a woodworker rushing over to help him smack on the nose. Tears welled up in the man's eyes, and all Salim could do was smile at him in embarrassment.

Instead of being ashamed at his own childish sport, Salim inwardly cursed the president, whom he held personally responsible for every pothole in the ancient city. Then he continued on his walk, with open eyes and a muddy right foot.

Inside the coppersmith shops the small chisels sounded as if they were chattering with the blank copper plates. While they left their marks on the copper cans and pots, the chisels themselves stayed blank, as if unimpressed by the tinny copper prattle. Salim stopped at one of the smallest booths, whose owner he knew well. The somewhat squat, fifty-year-old man recognized the old coachman right away. He left the tray he was working on, and hurried over to Salim. "Uncle Salim, what's this I hear? Junis told me the whole story. By my children's health, I've been worried sick about you. Come inside. Do me the honor and come inside for some coffee."

Salim went in with the man, who immediately sent an apprentice to a nearby café to bring the old coachman a mocha.

The small shop smelled of tar and burnt cloth. The coppersmith noticed the anxiety on the old coachman's face. "God has been merciful to me. My apprentice wanted to heat up the tar a little to keep the copper plate from nicks and dents, and in the process the curtain caught fire. I was sitting with my back to the shop and didn't smell a thing. I've had a cold for days. But God protected me and the bread of my children—probably because I took this orphan in as my apprentice." The craftsman grabbed Salim by the sleeve and looked around. "What kind of times are these?" he asked quietly. "Have you heard about the cholera up north? You I can tell this to. I heard about it from my cousin. He just came from there. Uncle, what kind of government is this that doesn't even tell its own people about a cholera epidemic? And why? So the tourists won't be scared away. God knows I'm not some frightened little rabbit; besides, it's all the same to me. I've lived long enough. But my six children! The poor children. For weeks now they haven't been allowed to buy any treats on the street, and we wash everything we eat with hot water and potassium permanganate. Maybe I'm overdoing it. Do you think there's an epidemic?"

Salim shrugged his shoulders and took the coffee that the apprentice was politely offering.

The old coachman slurped his mocha loudly and with delight; he set his cup down on the small table, then pointed to a magnificent, round copper platter and rubbed his thumb and forefinger together to indicate money, in order to find out the price.

"Just take it. I will give it to you!" the man declared.

Salim raised his bushy eyebrows the way Damascenes do to say no with the least possible amount of effort. Only Damascenes—so people say—could have come up with this particular brand of laziness, this method of saying no without even moving their head. The most diligent among Arabs actually say the word *no*. Those somewhat more inclined to comfort will raise their head and click their tongue. But the laziest of lazy Damascenes simply raise their eyebrows without a sound. And it was this manner that Salim followed his whole life long.

The coppersmith laughed with delight. "You like stories, don't you?" And since he well knew the coachman's vice, he went on without waiting for an answer: "You know the Englishman who lives next door and works in the museum? His name is Mister John. He used to be so worried about his beautiful wife that he would lock up the house whenever he went out. The women in our neighborhood, they all liked her and kept inviting her to coffee, but she just sat smiling by her window, sad and lonely. Her husband, he was afraid she might leave him. A month ago

he had to drive to Palmyra. They've dug up some more treasures there.

"Normally, when Mister John went away for any length of time, he always took his wife with him, but he didn't want to take her to Palmyra. There's a hotel there called Hotel Zenobia—you know about the beautiful Queen Zenobia who defied the Romans. Mister John was afraid of the legends surrounding this hotel. It had been founded by a rich Frenchwoman named Madame d'Andurian who fell in love with the desert, the Bedouins, and their Arabian horses. So Madame d'Andurian moved to Palmyra and had this hotel built. In its stables she kept Arabian horses of the best blood. Madame was very generous and often gave lavish banquets. Rumor had it that they were wild orgies. Tales of her charm and generosity quickly made the rounds, so libertines of all stripes—governors, politicians, generals, diplomats—they all traveled to Palmyra to be pampered by Madame d'Andurian. But Madame was not only admired; she was also hated. In time her name acquired a certain tinge of notoriety. Some people called her—perhaps out of jealousy—'the enchantress of the desert.'

"One day her husband was found murdered in a barn. You know how back then the French and English were fighting their secret spy wars all over the Middle East, to see who would wind up with all our riches. With all the horrible goings-on, spies and innocent people alike frequently disappeared without a

trace. I'm sure you remember the beautiful, the fabu-
lously beautiful singer Asmahan. Who could forget
her? Well, she was murdered as well—maybe she
knew too much, or maybe she wouldn't carry out an
assignment. Well, anyway, people whispered that the
English secret service did away with Madame d'Andurian's husband because he was a highly placed
French agent. But the English spread rumors that the
Frenchwoman had instructed her Bedouin lover to
murder him. In any case, from then on, all the well-
known personalities stayed away from the hotel, and
Madame was lonely to the point of suffocating. She,
the great Madame d'Andurian, was now all alone,
forsaken in the sand. She couldn't stand it for long.
One day she decided to buy a sailing ship, and she
sailed the seven seas until a mutiny broke out among
her crew. By then Madame was quite old, and there
was little her charm could do to save the situation.
But she stuck to her guns—literally—and charged the
mutineers all by herself, brandishing a small pistol.
The seamen simply picked her up and threw her
overboard. They heard her crying out 'Zenobia!
Zenobia!' until the waves devoured her.

"Well, Mister John also knew the story of Queen
Zenobia, who is said to have had her husband, King
Odenathus, murdered so that she would inherit the
crown. And being the good Englishman, he probably
believed that it was a Bedouin who killed Madame
d'Andurian's husband. He feared the Bedouins even

more than he mistrusted the Damascenes, and so he decided to leave his beautiful wife at home. He lied to her and told her there was no hotel in Palmyra, that he and his workers would have to make do with tents and sleep on the hard ground. Mister John bought a week's supply of food for his wife—that was how long he planned to be away—and locked her in. He warned her never to speak with Arabs and she answered him 'Yes, yes,' and 'No, no,' the way the English do.

"Meanwhile the women in the neighborhood had conspired to have a key made for Mister John's door. They took the woman into their midst and plucked out all the little hairs on her legs, the way our women do. Then they all had great fun. Not only did they teach her Arabian dances, they also instructed her how to deceive men with her cunning. Uncle, the things they say in these circles about us men, it's enough to turn your hair gray!

"One week later, the Englishman came back and found his wife—how shall I say?—somewhat changed. She was sassy to him and very cheery. She showed off her legs and made fun of his pale face.

"Mister John was stricken with concern. 'Have you been talking to the Arabs?' he asked. His wife just looked at him without saying a word . . . and slowly raised her eyebrows."

Salim laughed with pleasure, frightening the artisan with his noiseless guffaws.

"Let's say twenty liras," the coppersmith said casually. "In the Hamadiya bazaar they sell the same platter for fifty. They buy theirs from me."

Salim took another sip, put the cup on the table, and used his fingers to show he would only pay ten liras.

"Uncle, that's too little. I'd rather give it to you. There's a whole day of work in a platter like that. Look here at the woman's face. She's practically talking to you. And damask roses like these, do you know how much work is in each leaf?"

Salim nodded and bid eleven liras.

"That copper comes from America. I pay twice as much as the others do for their cheap tins that start streaking blue and green after one week. Here's something that will last you for life, fifteen liras, my final word."

Salim raised his eyebrows, stuck obstinately to his eleven, and stood up. He started to leave.

"No, I don't want you to go empty-handed. Give me thirteen." And without waiting for the coachman's answer, he called back into the shop: "Ismail, come over here! Wrap up this pretty platter for Uncle Salim."

Salim took out his coin purse and handed the apprentice twelve liras, rubbing each one between his fingers before giving it away, as if he were afraid his government pension was escaping his company all too quickly.

"*Mabruk!* Blessed be the tea you serve on this platter," said the apprentice, handing the package to Salim. The coachman smiled and gave him two piasters. Then he turned around, pointed to the empty cup, and nodded his thanks for the coffee. He was visibly pleased with the bargain. The tooth of time had nibbled all the color from his old tea tray.

The street grew narrower and narrower, and the warning cries of the porters sounded louder and louder. "Watch out, man, make room!" "Watch out, make way!" "Watch out, ma'am!" They shouted and laboriously snaked their way with their unwieldy loads through the sea of people that grew denser and denser the closer Salim came to the spice market. The old coachman, too, had to strain to find his way through the ringing of the bicycles, the honking of the carts, and the cries of vendors, porters, and beggars, and although it was quite cold, he began to sweat.

When Salim reached the spice market, he took a short rest in a tiny café. The tables were just large enough for a cup of coffee, a glass of water, and an ashtray—nothing more. The only person seated inside was a man with gray hair and a stubbly beard who seemed to be a friend of the owner. The private conversation died down as soon as Salim walked in. The old coachman was just able to catch the word

Mazzah—the prison for "politicals." "It's colder today than it was yesterday," the proprietor repeated from time to time and thoughtfully ran his fingers over the amber beads of his rosary.

Salim drank his coffee slowly and looked through the steamed-up windows at the people hurrying by on their way to the market. An old horse stopped in front of the café. Despite the cold the horse was dripping with sweat and panting loudly as it tugged away at the heavy cart: a wheel was stuck in a deep pothole. The young driver cursed and whipped the horse without mercy. Salim tensed up and shook his head, and not until some passersby helped pull the cart, heavily loaded with bulging sacks, out of the pothole did the old coachman feel relieved.

When Salim left the café, he was enveloped in an aromatic cloud that came wafting from the spice market. Star anise, cardamom, and coriander were crassly celebrating their triumph over all the other spices, though thyme from the Syrian mountains kept chiming in as well with its deep voice and a stubbornness impossible to ignore. Now and then cinnamon would whisper sweetly and seductively, when the master spices weren't paying attention. Only the saffron blossoms kept silent, preferring to rely solely on their radiant yellow to entice prospective buyers.

Lies and spices are siblings. A lie can change even the blandest occurrence into a piquant dish. The truth

and nothing but the truth is something only a judge wants to hear. But just like spices, lies should be used solely to add a little flavor. "Not too little, not too much," thought Salim, "that's how they're best savored." He paused for a moment at the entrance to the bathhouse and looked over at the shops whose shelves were filled to the brim with spices.

It had been years since Salim had taken a steam bath. He bathed every Saturday in his kitchen using an ancient tin basin. He had just managed to take a couple of steps inside when he was jostled by a young man wearing nothing but a towel. The man gave a shriek—he was running from another man who was hot on his heels with a bucket of icy water. The place was crowded with soldiers; they had occupied all the benches in the tearoom. Salim recognized them by their short hair. The room reeked of sweat, and that repulsed the old coachman. It seemed the men had never been to the baths before; they were making as much noise as they would at a fairground. Gone was the peace and quiet so treasured by every connoisseur of the steam bath. Salim could hear them shouting for hand towels. He had never heard such a thing in all his years, for the attendants always provided more than enough towels for their guests the moment they began undressing. "They must be enlisted men or very young officers," he thought, and hurried out, just as the two young men who had raced past a

moment before started wrestling on the ground in front of the fountain, to the great amusement and applause of their comrades.

Salim suddenly felt hungry. Not far from the bath two vendors were selling kebabs, grilled innards, boiled tongue, and roasted liver. They were hawking their wares loudly and aggressively. "Walk up and have a taste before I sell out!" shouted one. "You don't need a single tooth to eat mine!" countered the other, "the meat's so tender it'll melt on your tongue!" Many passersby let themselves be tempted—the spice market had already set their mouths to watering. Salim listened to the loud offers and decided on the man who was loudly proclaiming his generous use of fresh parsley. Since Salim wanted to pamper himself he purchased three kebab sticks for one lira. But he was only able to enjoy one. Not because the vendor had been exaggerating: no, the fresh parsley really did make the kebab taste delicious. But then, on top of a table inside the shop, he saw two boiled sheep heads. The one on the right was munching a bunch of parsley; his tongue was hanging from his mouth at a particularly odd angle. The other one was grinning right at Salim, showing off his mighty maw. Clutching his kebabs, Salim turned and looked down at the ground, but there he saw a third mutton head beneath the butcher's block, in the middle of the offal. It had yet to be boiled and was gazing up at Salim with large, reproachful eyes and a dangling tongue. Salim

wrapped the two kebabs in some pita bread and hurried away; he felt an unbearable, burning pressure in his stomach. He waited for the fresh air to cool off his head. Salim hunkered down in front of a spice shop and hastily devoured the kebabs with the bread. But they no longer tasted very good.

After his meal he made his way through the goldsmiths' market to the Umayyad Mosque.

A remarkable calm emanated from the great hall of the mosque. The people walked noiselessly across the floor covered with heavy Persian rugs, lost in thought or engrossed in silent prayer. Or else they sat in a group around a learned elder, talking. Others were sleeping or staring intently at a point in the high dome, at an ornament hanging on the wall or from the ceiling.

Salim's legs were sore, and the fatty meat made his stomach heavy. He stretched out on a rug and wondered why he had recently felt this emptiness inside his head. Never in his life had he had such difficulty thinking his thoughts through as in the last months. They were becoming more and more blurred— probably because he was no longer able to speak with anyone. So the tongue, he reasoned, is like a potter's hands, which give the clay such beautiful and useful form. Salim smiled at the droll insight that he could think clearly only if he talked. And just as that thought was taking shape, he saw his wife coming around the corner. He rubbed his eyes in amazement.

Zaida was walking toward him wearing a blue velvet dress and smiling. Her delicate fingers had the red tint of henna. Her hair was gray, but it had a reddish cast. She laughed when she saw him. "What are you doing here, my Salim, little tassel of my heart? Why are you sleeping here?"

"My legs were a little tired. I'm not as young as I used to be, you know. In the old days I used to make it from our street to the mosque in an hour; today it took me three times as long."

"You've just become a tortoise, my Salim, and like a tortoise you're going to live to be a hundred. Didn't I tell you? Once, when you were very sick, the angel of death came to me. 'Well, old woman,' said the cutter of all souls, 'I'll be coming for him soon, and you'll be looking for someone else.' But I haggled with him until he finally took ten years from my life and gave them to you. He called me a crazy woman and hurried to Abdullah the goldsmith. Didn't I tell you the very next morning, how Abdullah had died in the night? You just laughed at me. 'Abdullah? You're crazy, the angel of death won't get far with him. That man has seven souls, just like a cat.' Isn't that what you said? And then what happened? Abdullah lay dead in his bed. His widow's still alive and doing well. The reason so many wives outlive their husbands is because they aren't so foolish as to take life as seriously as their spouses. But I *wanted* to die first. I was always bored when you were away, and I

couldn't stand being bored. That's all. Don't look at me so horrified. I know, I know, not a second went by when you weren't head over heels in love with me. I, on the other hand, found life with you to be very stressful, but never boring. Isn't that love enough? What a beautiful tray."

"I just bought it today. Ours was getting much too old." No sooner had Salim spoken these words than Afifa and two other women strode into the mosque.

"Give it to me, I'll make some coffee for the guests!" Zaida called out, but Salim roared, "No, not for Afifa!" Zaida tore the platter from his hand.

Salim woke up in fright. He clutched all around him. His platter had disappeared. He looked over to the people gathered around the learned man. They were still debating quietly, although a little more heatedly. Aha! Fighting over the booty! They sit there peacefully as can be, waiting until your eyes begin to droop, and then they make their move. A learned man and his students, my foot! More likely Ali Baba sitting with his forty thieves.

Salim jumped up and hurried out. How long had he been asleep? Where was his tray now? When he entered the yard of the mosque, he saw a circle of young people sitting in a distant corner. Two attendants were sweeping the perfectly spotless aisle with large palm leaves. Salim trotted behind them. But the young people had no tray. Salim tried asking them with his hands, but they only giggled in reply.

In a rage, Salim left the mosque and hurried home. His head was throbbing with self-reproach, as well as anger at the entire thieving world—of all the tea trays around, they had to choose his. He had never been the most pious man in Damascus, but in his ire he considered it absolutely shameless to steal in the house of God. His thoughts grew bleaker and bleaker and began to smell strongly of burning tar, although he was just crossing the spice market.

"Uncle, hey, Uncle!" he suddenly heard someone calling. He turned around. A boy was waving to him from the vicinity of the tiny café. He was holding up the platter, and Salim stared at him, practically in shock.

"Uncle, you disappeared so suddenly. This belongs to you, doesn't it?" asked the boy, who came running and gasping for air.

Salim nodded and held the boy, whose face was scarred with pockmarks, firmly by the hand until he dug a lira out of his bag. He handed him the coin.

"A whole lira! My heavens!" the boy cried and started dancing for joy right then and there. As Salim well knew, a café errand boy had to work a whole week to earn one lira. The coachman was ashamed he had suspected the learned elder. But Salim could never stay ashamed for very long. Soon enough he was feeling proud of the tea he would serve that evening on his brand-new tea tray. Pride was the best

shower he could take to wash away his feelings of guilt.

Salim hurried home, leaving the old bazaar behind him, and when he opened the door to his room late in the afternoon, the hustle and bustle of the old quarter had faded, and all its sights and sounds were woven into a distant whisper, as full of life and color and every bit as rugged as an Oriental rug.

7

*How
one man's
hunger for a dream
kept everyone else well fed*

People didn't know much about Junis, even though he had run his coffeehouse near the Bab Tuma for over thirty years. Everyone raved about his Yemenite coffee, his Lebanese arak, his Egyptian beans, and his pipe tobacco from Latakia, but hardly anyone knew where Junis himself had come from.

People did know that in the mid-thirties he bought a dilapidated old dive and expanded it into a coffee-house—and that he spared no expense in making it the most beautiful establishment in the Christian quarter. But he was jinxed. No sooner had he opened its doors than the magnificent coffeehouse burned down. Debts consumed ten years of his life before he again reached the point where he had been when the fire struck.

Junis was often morose, and almost always in a bad mood. People said he used to be as happy as a clown, but if anyone asked him where his good mood had gone, he would answer drily: "It burned away."

In addition to his bad mood, his excellent water-pipe, and his Yemenite mocha, he was known

throughout the quarter for his boiled beans. Stingy as
he was with everything else, Junis was remarkably
generous when it came to these beans. A few piasters
would buy a heaping plateful of this wonderfully filling, and terribly indigestible, dish. If the first serving
wasn't enough, all you had to do was walk up to the
counter, hold out your empty plate, and whisper,
"Adjustment." Without batting an eyelash, the cook
would dispense a second, even a third portion free of
charge—only an elephant could put away a fourth
"adjustment." In no other restaurant in Damascus—
or probably in all the world—did the word *adjustment*
have such a meaning.

The kitchen stopped serving in the early afternoon;
the late afternoon was reserved for waterpipes and tea;
and after the sun set, it was time for the hakawatis.
Night after night these storytellers climbed on a high
stool and entertained the guests with their gripping
tales of love and adventure. The listeners would talk
among themselves and interrupt the stories with their
comments and quarrels; at times they would even
demand that the hakawati repeat a passage they had
particularly enjoyed. The hakawatis, for their part,
had to compete with the noise. Interestingly, however, the more the suspense grew, the more quietly
the hakawati would tell the story. The listeners would
then admonish each other to be silent, so that they
could follow the plot. When the tale reached its most
dramatic moment—for instance, when the hero had

climbed up the trellis to his beloved and was hanging from her balcony by his fingertips—a watchman or father would inevitably appear on the scene. Here the hakawati would interrupt his tale and promise to continue the next evening. The storyteller did this so that the guests would come back to Junis' and not go to one of his competitors. Sometimes the listeners got so excited, they would descend on the hakawati, offer him a waterpipe or some tea, and discreetly ask him to give away the rest of the story. But no hakawati dared surrender the suspense; Junis had strictly forbidden them to do so. "Come back tomorrow and you'll find out what happens," was always their answer.

Damascenes tell many anecdotes about quarrels breaking out among the listeners, who often took sides with the characters in a tale. Some would stand by the bride's family; others insisted that the groom was in the right. There are other stories about listeners who were so curious or in such a state of suspense they couldn't sleep. In the middle of the night they would go to the hakawati's house and bribe him to let the hero into his beloved's chamber, or to arrange for the hero's escape from prison. Supposedly only a few hakawatis ever accepted such offers, and then never without first making the listeners swear they would come to the coffeehouse the next day, for by no means could Junis learn of their transaction.

. . .

When Junis arrived, Salim had just finished preparing the tea and the waterpipe. The old coachman not only seemed happy, he looked as if he had grown younger by a couple of decades.

"Were you in the steam bath?" asked Faris.

"Did you have a shave?" inquired Isam.

Salim shook his head. With two fingers of his right hand and the outstretched palm of his left, he showed that he had been out for a walk.

"What a beautiful tea tray, how much did it cost you?" the emigrant asked, admiring the new platter.

"More than twenty liras, that's for certain. Such fine handiwork," stated the minister.

"I could get that exact same tray for fifteen," said Isam, the most experienced haggler among them.

Salim nodded and was pleased with his bargain, which wasn't a true bargain unless everyone else thought he had paid more than he really had.

"So today it's your turn," the minister said to Junis. "But that shouldn't pose a problem for you. You must have heard and seen a thousand stories in your café."

"You're mistaken, my friend," replied the proprietor. "The guests don't tell many stories in the coffee-house; that's why we have the hakawati. He's a professional. Most guests, in fact, have precious little to say."

"That's the first time I've ever heard *that*," Faris contended. "I thought people went to the café day in and day out just to talk."

"Yes, that's what everybody thinks, but if you'd run a café for as many years as I did, you'd see I was right. At first it was fascinating to listen to all those people, but the fascination soon wore off, because, really, they all just repeat the same thing over and over. One man is constantly gabbing about his liver, the other is always going on about his unfortunate son. It makes no difference if someone starts talking about cucumbers, because the minute he does, the one with the liver is going to say: 'Cucumbers are bad for your liver. I should know. When my liver was still healthy . . .' and he's back on his subject. Meanwhile, the one with the unhappy son isn't paying the least bit of attention; he's looking out for the slightest opportunity and waiting for a cue that would allow him to start back in on his son. Some people never really talk about anything—they just repeat the same old sentence from time to time. And then I had one customer from up north who came every day and drank exactly five glasses of arak—never four and never six. He would down his first glass in complete silence, but from the second glass on, he was absolutely certain to start composing these stupid rhymes."

"You're never satisfied with anything, are you!" Tuma jabbed.

"You should have heard him: 'Cheers, Junis!' he would shout, holding up his second glass. 'I'll drink to Tunis!' "

"And with his third glass," Isam laughed, "Cheers Ali! I'll drink to Mali!"

"Yes, that's about the size of it. Every night he would begin with me and end with some major capital. So you can see how much my customers really had to say. Even so, it was a paradise compared to today, when no one so much as opens his mouth inside the café. They just sit there dumber than fish and listen to the goddamn radio. At first I thought the radio was a blessing for coffeehouses. I even bought one myself, an expensive one, so I could have some music now and then. But ever since the new regime flooded the market with those portable transistor radios for a measly ten liras, nobody talks in the café anymore. In the old days, if there were twenty people sitting in my place, there were twenty prophets. Everyone spoke his mind out loud and no one was afraid of anything. Today you can't tell a joke without someone giving you the evil eye and asking who you meant by 'idiot' or 'jackass.' Anything you want to say, you have to protect yourself first. You have to listen to the latest news, so you'll know whom the regime has just declared friend or foe.

"Yesterday I was at my son's bar. I've been so worried about Salim that I haven't listened to the news in weeks. Well, my son brought me some tea, and I started telling him about my youngest sister. She's married to a Lebanese and has been living in

Beirut for forty years. All of a sudden this total stranger butts in and says in a loud voice, 'I wouldn't let my sister marry some Lebanese dog!' My son whispered that the man was from the secret police and that our president had declared Lebanon an enemy country. I had no idea. I was so mad I was boiling over, and I was ready to whack this loudmouth a few times with my cane, to teach him not to insult his elders—but my son begged me not to. 'That would ruin me,' he said, 'they'd shut down the place within hours.' Someone would plant a handful of hashish somewhere, you see, or else a book by Lenin. The police would show up an hour later, and they'd find the hashish and the Lenin exactly where the man from the secret police had stashed them. The place would be closed and its proprietor thrown in prison for ten or twenty years.

"How in the hell are people supposed to talk to each other with all that? The only thing I knew about the mess in Lebanon was that there was fighting. Is that any reason for me to disown my sister?"

Faris, the former statesman, felt uneasy. The coachman's small room had a window facing the street, and although it was icy cold outside, the louder Junis spoke, the more uneasy he became. And that night, Junis was quite agitated and loud. Faris gave Tuma a wink, and the latter nodded, as if to say that he had understood.

"But the hakawatis, they told stories, didn't they? What kind of stories were they?" he asked Junis.

"Oh they told stories all right," said Junis. "I must have heard thousands of them. You know, I had quite a few storytellers over the years. Well, last night was the first time I ever thought long and hard about my hakawatis. Many were bad, but a few were good. Anyone who bored his listeners was bad.

"A story had to taste every bit as good as the food, otherwise most of my guests would get up, pay for their waterpipe, and leave; after all, they could bore themselves at home for less money. It was a bad hakawati who couldn't tell when his listeners were bored. But you know, what amazed me was that the good hakawatis didn't have flying carpets constantly whizzing around, or dragons spitting fire, or witches concocting crazy potions. They kept their listeners just as spellbound with the simplest things. But there's one thing that even a bad hakawati has to have—a good memory. He can never get so worried or carried away that he loses the thread. This doesn't mean his memory has to be as amazing as our Salim's, but it's got to be pretty good, or else he's lost."

"My God, if that's all you need," the barber chimed in.

"Just a minute now. Sometimes I can't even remember what I said two days ago," the locksmith said and laughed.

"No, Musa's right," said the emigrant. "The whole world knows that all Arabs are born with a good memory. They never forget a thing, and that's why they love the camel. A camel doesn't forget anything, either. But it's not always a gift; sometimes it can be a curse. Do you know the story of Hamad?"

"No, but it's not your turn today," the teacher protested.

"Let him tell the story," Isam requested. "I'd like to find out how a good memory can also be a curse. But only if it's all right with Junis, of course—after all, it's his night."

Junis smiled. "Go ahead. We're not in school."

"Okay," Tuma began, "so once there was this farmer named Hamad. One day the village elder was preparing to marry off his only daughter. The wedding celebrations were going to last for seven days and seven nights. The bride's father invited all the people in the village; his generosity knew no bounds. The first night there was roast lamb, aromatic rice, beans, and a salad with onions and garlic. Everything tasted delicious. The guests were enjoying the bountiful feast, and Hamad, who had gone hungry half his life, overdid it. Within two hours he devoured an entire leg of lamb, a huge bowl of rice, and an even bigger bowl of salad.

"Okay, so—late in the night Hamad started having a terrible attack of gas. He was sitting on the floor in the banquet room, and when the gas became unbearable, he tried to get up and go outside to fart, but just as he was standing up he passed wind so loudly it roared. This happened at the very moment the poet was reciting his verse in praise of the bride's grace and charm, and precisely at the line 'Your breath is like a whiff of jasmine!' The people laughed, but the host threw Hamad a look that could annihilate. You know, a guest may sooner stab his host with a knife than fart or burp at his table. And yet, in other parts of the world, a host counts himself lucky if his guest happens to burp."

"Those people must be complete idiots," said Junis. "At any rate, no one in my café would even dare imagine such a thing."

"Well, you know, other countries, other customs," said the emigrant, coming to the defense of burpers of all lands.

"No, it's not proper. Next thing you know, they'll say 'Bless you' whenever you fart," Ali protested.

"Come on, let Tuma finish his story, or else we'll never get to Junis," Faris spoke up.

"Okay, as I was saying, Hamad was so ashamed that he ran out. For days he was so ridiculed, both by the children and the adults in his village, that he couldn't stand it. He packed his things and left for Brazil. At that time there were many Arabs who emigrated to America. Some because they were starving; others, like me, because they were persecuted; and Hamad, just because he had farted.

"He worked abroad for forty years. It's a hard life, I can tell you. Still, Hamad managed to build up a modest fortune. One day he was overcome with longing to see his village, and he paid a mint to travel from Brazil to Syria. As soon as he laid eyes on the fields of his village, he asked the bus driver to stop. Hamad wanted to smell the earth of his home—you know, return to the village on foot, just as he had left it. He strode slowly toward the village, enjoying the fresh air and constantly bending down to touch the earth. When he reached the village cemetery, he was seized with curiosity. He wanted to know who had died while he was away. So he went in and wandered from one grave to the next, reading the names of the deceased and praying for their souls. Then he saw the gravestone of one of his best childhood friends. He was more than a little amazed, since this friend had always been the picture of health. There was no date on the gravestone. An elderly woman was tending a small grave nearby. Hamad went over to her. He didn't know her. 'Salaam aleikum, Grandmother. I've just come back from Brazil and see that Ismail has died. His gravestone's almost gone to ruin. Can you tell me when he died?'

" 'I can tell you that exactly,' answered the old lady. 'Ismail died two years to the day after Hamad's Fart. His wife died three years later.'

"Hamad shrieked like a madman and hurried back to Brazil."

"A lovely story, but don't you think it's time we heard Junis?" suggested the teacher.

"I forget where I left off," said the café owner.

"You were talking about how the hakawatis have to have a good memory," Isam reminded him.

"That's right, a hakawati has to have that. But I also wanted to say that their profession is very hard work. I saw it night after night. The hakawatis would walk off the stage as exhausted as heavy laborers. And they earned very little. When I paid them, I sometimes asked: 'Why do you tell stories all evening for so little money.' Some said: 'We never learned to do anything else. Our grandfathers and our fathers were hakawatis.' But one day one of the best storytellers I ever had answered me like this: 'My listeners pay me very well,' he said, 'and no gold in the world can equal the happiness of seeing this miracle take place in their eyes, as full-grown savage lions turn into meek and eager children.'

"Well, I thought long and hard about what I would tell Salim tonight, and all of you. Naturally I've held on to a few of the stories my hakawatis told, but on the way over I felt this desire to tell you about myself. We've been friends for over ten years, and you hardly know anything about my life. It's a strange enough story.

"Well, I don't know when I was born. My mother said it was a very hot day. I was the youngest of ten children."

"Please, wait just a minute," Faris said and hurried out to the toilet. Ali seized the opportunity to throw two large pieces of wood in the oven, and Tuma put on his glasses.

When Faris came back, he stood beside the oven and rubbed his frozen hands. Junis took a tin of snuff from his vest pocket, carefully tapped a small heap of tobacco in the hollow above his left thumb, and inhaled it deeply, moving his head back and forth. Then he wiped his nose with his large handkerchief and leaned back.

"Well," Junis began again after Faris had sat down, "we lived in Harasta, which in those days was still a tiny village. My father was a poor stonemason. I shared a small room with my nine siblings: six boys and three girls. We had only one other room, which was used as a kitchen during the day and served as a bedroom for my parents at night. I didn't have a happy childhood. Of course, I'm experiencing one now, with my grandchildren . . .

"Well, back then we had to get up at four o'clock almost every day. My three oldest brothers had to go to the building site with my father to learn his trade. One brother was apprenticed to a butcher, another to a baker, and a third worked for a knife grinder—and they all earned next to nothing. The girls had to help out at home as soon as they could stand on their own two legs.

"The school was a horror. An old imam taught us

more about kicks and canings than about the Koran. Still, my father never gave up the hope that one of his sons might become an imam. He wasn't religious, but any family that provided the mosque with its imam earned great respect in the village. So he sent me to the horrible old man. But just like my brothers, I didn't last more than two years. It was a bitter defeat for my father, and since I was his youngest son, I was also his final disappointment. He never spoke to me from that day on. Never again. For years he never answered when I greeted him; he treated me like I was air. As far as he was concerned I didn't exist. He wouldn't even beat me. That's how much this final disappointment had hurt him.

"I didn't really care what was going to become of me—all I knew was that I didn't want to go back to the imam. I would rather have died. The decrepit old man acted as if he would live forever; he didn't want any of his pupils to advance. When the reaper of all souls finally came for him, among the three thousand inhabitants of our village it was impossible to find a single young man who could read the Koran respectably. That's how bad this imam really was. They had to bring someone in from Duma in order to keep the mosque going. The new imam had a gentle demeanor but a voracious appetite. All the chickens in the village would gladly have emigrated to America if they could. But that's another story.

"Well, my father had leased a field for a small

amount of money in order to raise wheat and vegetables to keep the family fed. My three sisters, my mother, and I had to do all the work. Winter was the only time we could rest. From spring on we had to get up every morning before the sun rose to work the field. All day long we pulled weeds, planted the rows, and watered them over and over. When the vegetables were ripe, we all worked together harvesting the eggplants, zucchinis, tomatoes, and cucumbers.

"One crate of vegetables a day was all we could manage. I had to go to market by myself. My father didn't want the girls to go there, although women and young girls often sold things at the market. At first I carried the heavy crate on my head, but then I scrounged together two wheels and a metal rod and fixed them so I could pull the crate behind me. From then on, going to market was fun. I enjoyed selling the vegetables, and the market was so full of life it helped me forget how exhausted I was from the field work. Sometimes in the summer, if I made a good sale, I treated myself to an ice cream. That was like a holiday meal for me. First I would wash my hands and face at the fountain, then walk over to the ice cream vendor and with a loud voice order an ice cream. 'Sir,' I would call out, 'may your hand be guided by a generous heart, for my half-piaster is honestly earned!' The ice cream vendors would laugh with pleasure and give me an extra spoonful.

"Although I was often dead tired, I hardly ever fell asleep tending my goods, but once I did nod off, and someone stole an eggplant.

"Well, there was one thing I hated worse than the plague, I can tell you, and that was the wheat harvest. The cutter's work is a living hell for back and hands. The cut wheat had to be carried to the village threshing floor and threshed there. We had no good sickles and no good rope; we didn't even have a donkey—although I would have preferred to be one myself so I wouldn't feel the pain so much. The damned chaff burned my eyes and throat. The sun beat down on us without mercy. I would have given the world for a little bit of shade and a drop of cool water.

"My mother was often sick. She was sick the whole time I knew her, but she wouldn't hear of our going out into the field alone, and even when she was so frail she could barely walk, she would sit in the middle of the field and sing us songs, to cheer us up a little. They were funny songs, and I can remember we sometimes laughed so hard we cried. We were concerned for her health and always pleaded with her to stay home, but she didn't want to leave us alone. 'As long as I can see, I want to fill my eyes with the sight of you,' was the way she always answered.

"After the harvest she would go with us to the threshing floor and sit there despite the heat. There wasn't a single tree on the hill where the village did its threshing. When one of us children grew tired we could go to her and lay our head in her lap for a little while. She would bend over us and shade us.

"My mother died in the spring of the year I turned twelve. I ran around the fields like mad, screaming out loud for her. I cried and cried and cursed heaven. I stayed outside in the fields. Today I'm sure that the pain I felt that night made me crazy for a while. The next morning I started running; I ran through villages I had never seen before. I stopped people on the street and asked, 'Do you really think my mother's dead?' Most people just pushed me away, but finally someone took me in, although who it was I have no more idea today than I did then. The only thing I remember is being terribly afraid of the way the room looked, with this dim oil lamp glowing and flickering. It was practically empty—just a mattress and a stool—and the ceiling had a large, strangely crooked beam running through the center. I sat huddled in a corner and stared at the beam for a long time before I fell asleep. I don't know when I came back to our village, half starved and completely filthy. My sisters said that it was a month after our mother's death.

"When it came time to harvest the wheat that year, I built a small tent of twigs and foliage on the threshing floor, which my sisters and I called 'Mother.'

"Well, my oldest sister had married at the age of sixteen, shortly before my mother's death. The second-oldest was fifteen at the time and had to take care of the household all alone. That left the youngest of my sisters—who was only one year older than I was—and myself to do all the work in the field. It was my job to turn the wheat and guard it until sunset. Then my father would relieve me, without saying a word, and spend the night on the threshing floor. Unbelievable! He would come, sit down, and stare into the distance. I would always kiss his hand, but he would shove me away and wipe off the back of his hand. Every day I was very fearful of our meeting, and every day, when I kissed his hand, he would shove me away.

"The wheat took time to dry; one rainshower meant putting the threshing off for days. We had to keep watch over the wheat around the clock, until it was safely stored in sacks inside our house. Times were very bad; people were starving. We heard the wildest stories about thieves stealing wheat in broad daylight, while the farmer was taking his midday nap

"I had to stay with the threshing the whole day. But a few boys from the village who were somewhat better off met every day and took a short hike to the village spring. I watched them go, and inside I was boiling over with envy and rage because I was not allowed to play with them.

"Well, once I saw the boys sitting around the village spring. My sister was in a good mood that day. She let me go down to the boys and play for an hour. When I reached the spring, they were sitting in a circle, drinking tea that they had made over a small fire and taking turns telling stories.

"I sat down beside the boys, and sooner or later it was my turn and I started to tell a nice story. They just laughed. 'We don't want to hear a story, we want to hear what you dreamt last night!' I was terrified—I had never even heard the word *dream* before. It took me some time to figure out why each one began his story with the words *I was* . . . I told the children that I had never dreamed.

" 'No wonder!' said the son of the village elder. 'How could you have, you poor devil. You sleep ten to a room, and you're up at the crack of dawn. A dream needs time and space!' I'll never forget those words as long as I live. That night I couldn't sleep. I took my blanket and sneaked out of the room. I went to the threshing floor, and lay down next to my father. He didn't notice anything, but that night I dreamt for the first time in my life. When I woke up, my father had already gone off to work. But I felt different the whole day, and from then on I was glad that I could dream just like the other boys. Night after night I would sneak off to my father, and one morning I was awakened by the stubble of his beard as he kissed me. He hugged me tightly to his breast and cried.

"On that day the world became a piece of heaven. Before noon I had turned the wheat three times. You didn't have to do it that often, once in the afternoon was enough. But a new power was flowing through my veins. And then came the catastrophe.

"The children came as usual to play at the spring, and waved to me to join them. I was afraid of leaving the wheat unattended. My sister had to help with the wash that day, so I was alone. My fear held me back, but my joy at the dreams I could tell the boys kept drawing me to them. I felt torn in two. Well, finally, when I saw them sitting in a circle, my desire won out. I went over to them, sat down, and told them several dreams. The children were fascinated. They said my dreams were wilder than anything they had ever dreamed.

"Well, after I had listened to the dreams of the other boys, I said goodbye and walked slowly back. You had to cross through a large vineyard and then spiral up the bald hill like around a snail's house. It was then I remembered the wheat. I looked up, but I couldn't see the large pile that had covered the middle of our floor. First I thought I had confused our floor with another, but then I recognized the tent I had made, the one we called 'Mother,' standing on the bare floor. My heart was pounding, and my legs began to wobble. I ran as fast as I could. When I reached the floor, I almost died: not a single hull was left. The neighbors all said they hadn't noticed a thing. They hurried with me to our place and couldn't believe their eyes. We looked far and wide but saw neither beast nor rider. For a long time I just

121

sat there and cried, until finally, before the sun went down, I left. I couldn't bear to face my father.

"I had no idea where to go. I started off toward Damascus until at last it got dark. Then I saw a coachman who was still trying to make it to Damascus, despite the late hour. He was goading his horses on and they were galloping like mad. I ran after the coach and with one great leap was able to grab on to the back bar. The coachman could tell that someone was hanging on his coach. But he didn't have time to stop and look, so he just cracked his whip in back of him, and that goddamn whip was long and hit my arms and legs like spears of fire. Never again did I see a whip as long as that. He kept on flogging both his horses and me. More than anything I wanted to jump off, but the ground beneath me had turned into a whirring grindstone. Whenever I tried to put my foot down, the road tore open my naked toes. The whip was searing me from above and the road from below. It was a hell. When the coach reached Damascus, my arms were bleeding. I climbed down, staggered away on shaky legs, and cursed the bones of this coachman's ancestors.

"Well, I'll keep it short, so as not to bore you," said Junis, looking at his friends.

"For God's sake, go on, in as much detail as you can!" replied Faris, and as if he had spoken the minds of the others, they all nodded and mumbled in accord.

"Your words are scarce drops of water, and we are like the thirsty earth," Mehdi the teacher exaggerated, and laughed at his own words.

"Well, all right. That night I soon found a place to stay. There was a blind man sitting in front of a courtyard; I greeted him as I walked by. Then the blind man returned my greeting and—God is my witness—he asked me why I was so hurt. I told him about my ordeal, and he cursed the heartless coachman, and gave me water and some salve from a small pot to lessen the pain. He let me spend the night on a small mattress in his room.

"The blind man had a box that he carried from a strap around his neck, and which contained everything from thimbles to candy. He was already very old, but when I told him the next day that I would be glad to do his selling for him, he declined. Earning money wasn't what made him happy, he said, but helping people in need did. This blind man was a strange fellow. I stayed with him for three days. Each day he left at dawn and didn't return until late. He was very excited when he told me how happy a woman on the other side of Damascus had been to discover that he had the very button she had been looking for for years. He kept a large tin box full of buttons. Whenever he found old, ragged clothes, he would cut off the buttons. He had a thousand colorful buttons and was as proud of them as if they had been Solomon's treasure.

"Well, after three days I thanked that good man and went on my way. I loafed about the city for weeks. Vowing never to return home, I swore to myself that I would either make it on my own or end like a dog—but I never wanted to see the sadness and bitter disappointment in my father's eyes again.

"I started hanging around the Hamadiya market; there was a real battle for every inch of space. Naturally, as a newcomer I received the worst spot, right across from a tailor's: the only other shops nearby sold various odds and ends like yarn, needles, stationery, ice cream—in any case, things that rarely required carrying. The stronger boys got the coveted places in front of the stores that sold furniture, cloth, and dishes.

"But one day I was lucky and saw this man coming out of the tailor's shop carrying a large packet. He was dressed finely and had the look of a wealthy gentleman. I hurried over and offered my services. 'I'll lighten your load for half a piaster, sir!' I called out, as I had learned from the other children who, like me, were hanging around the bazaar.

"Well, that was over sixty years ago, but to this day I don't know whether I met an angel, a devil, or both in one person. I accompanied the man home. He lived on Lazarists Street—just a few doors down from Tuma—in a small villa. I carried the packet to his home, and when we arrived he asked me how much

I wanted. A half-piaster would have been plenty, but to suggest a fixed amount would have been stupid. I had also learned from the children how to answer. 'Whatever your generosity permits,' I said. He liked that, and asked me where I came from. I joked that I was an exiled prince from the Sahara now working as an errand boy to earn enough money to buy horses and hire warriors. He laughed and gave me some food, and a glass of rose water to drink. Then he asked whether I knew how to read. I enjoyed joking around with him. I answered: 'Yes, but I would be ashamed to show my writing to you, O sir.'

" 'Ashamed?' he said. 'One is never ashamed to show that one can write, boy. Writing is a noble art. Show me how you can write!'

" 'Sir, it will hurt you!' I answered.

" 'It doesn't matter. Show me!'

"First I asked for my pay, since I didn't know how he would react. He gave me four piasters, which at that time was as much as a worker earned for a full day's work. 'Now I'm anxious to know how your writing is supposed to hurt!' he said, laughing.

"I kicked him in the behind. 'That's *A*,' I said. Then I hit him in the stomach. 'And that's how you write *B*.'

" 'What's that supposed to mean?' he asked in horror.

" 'Didn't I tell you, O sir. That's the language I

learned from the old imam. I know perfectly which beating goes with which letter, but I can't write a single one.'

"Instead of getting angry, he gazed at me with sad eyes. Then he paced up and down, examined me with an earnest expression, and shook his head. I drank the sweet rose water in silence, and was a little ashamed of my patched rags and naked feet. 'And would you like, O prince, to tarry in my humble abode until you have gathered enough gold for your horses and riders?' I heard his voice and couldn't believe my ears. Even today I have to cry when I think of it . . ." Junis' voice was choked with tears.

Salim stood up quickly and handed him the water jug. Junis drank one swallow and calmed down a little. "That of all the people in the world I had to deliver this man up to the hangman grieves me to this day."

"Tell us about it, and lighten your heart," Mehdi said, taking Junis by the arm. "Tell us!" he begged quietly, while Ali gently stroked the café owner on the back.

"From that day on I lived with Omar—that was his name. He had good clothes made for me and sent me to school. At first I didn't know anything about him. A housekeeper came every day, cooked, cleaned, and did the wash, and Omar paid her well. He lived alone and chose not to marry. I was allowed to go everywhere in the house except the cellar. When after a few weeks I asked him where his money came from, he answered, 'From my gold mine,' and laughed like a devil.

"Once I woke up in the middle of the night. Since it was very hot, I went into the small courtyard to cool off. I saw a light burning inside his cellar, so I crept down the stairs and peeped through the keyhole. There I saw him, sitting at a table, pouring glowing metal into a mold. Next he took out a shiny piece of metal that looked as round and golden as a gold lira, and filed it and polished it for a long time.

"The next day I told him I knew all about his gold mine. He was shocked, but I assured him that I was a deep well, and asked him why he had made only the one gold lira.

" 'One gold lira is enough for one week, and no one will ever find out,' he answered. For anyone but Omar one gold lira would have been enough for a whole month back then. It turned out he had obtained the finely crafted mold as well as the recipe for the brilliant mixture from an old master counterfeiter who had lived off this craft his entire life; every week he had poured one gold lira and then spent it in a different place. Omar, too, kept traveling north and south to exchange his fake gold liras for real money, and, like the master, he never poured two coins.

"I thought it was stupid. I told him he should make

hundreds of them, trade them in, and then retire. 'That way I'd never make it to retirement, my boy,' he answered.

"Well, the years I lived with Omar were the most wonderful years of my life. He was a father and a friend to me, until the day I divulged the secret to a schoolmate. This boy told me we ought to make a gold lira for ourselves every day and sell it somewhere else. Syria was big enough to handle two fake gold liras, and Omar wouldn't suspect a thing. At first I refused, but this damned devil kept pushing me more and more, until finally I agreed to try just one gold coin. So one day, when Omar was away, my schoolmate and I sneaked inside the cellar. We heated up the yellow alloy and poured it into the mold. The gold lira came out looking shabby, and I was afraid, but my friend said that he knew a dealer who was so greedy he'd buy anything, as long as it was cheap.

"Well, two days later, the police not only surrounded the house, they occupied the whole street. They arrested Omar and carried off his entire workshop from the cellar. When an officer asked him rudely what son of a whore had taught him to do that, Omar answered with a smile, 'The Sultan.'

"The next day I hurried to the Damascus prison to see him, but since he was being held as a traitor, he was forbidden to speak with anyone until his sentencing half a year later. I had fake papers made up to change my name and show that I was his nephew—

since then I've been called Junis. As a relative, I was the first one allowed to see him. I was trembling at the idea of meeting him, but he just beamed at me. I told him I was ashamed to death to have betrayed the one man in Damascus who had given me his love, that I would rather die than see him languish here in prison. Omar laughed. 'Instead of dying and being ashamed for the rest of your life,' he told me, 'you should use your head and learn: never tell everything you know.'

"Every day I visited him and brought him fruits and snuff. In order to bring him things without being searched, I had to bribe a series of guards. He secretly gave me letters to deliver to various addresses in Damascus. They were all elegant homes, and from them I received answers, which I would smuggle back into the prison. I was exhausted, since at the time I was working in a large café where I waited on tables for very little money. I saved every piaster of my wages and tips. I stole from the owner whenever I could, and bought Omar fruits and snuff.

After a month, Omar asked me what I intended to do with myself. I answered: 'I'm not thinking about myself until you're out of here.'

" 'I will be out of here in ten days,' he answered with a laugh. 'So, then, what will you do with yourself eleven days from now?'

" 'I'd like to open a café.'

" 'Now listen closely to me. Go down into the cellar and you'll find a big marble slab underneath the wood stove. Lift it up and you'll find a box. Inside this box are two sacks, a big one, filled with hay, which belongs to me, and a small one, in which you'll find two hundred gold liras of the best counterfeit. No man on earth can tell them from the real thing. You'll be safe from the slightest suspicion. They're yours, if you promise me you'll never let any guest leave your café hungry or dissatisfied. Ten days from now is Thursday, understand? On Thursday night, bring the sack of hay to the coffeehouse next to the fountain near the Umayyad Mosque. Sit in the first row, listen to the hakawati's story, and then leave. God have mercy on you if you can't keep this to yourself. And woe to you if you open the sack of hay. I will kill you. Do you hear? Kill you.'

"I hurried home and shoved the marble slab aside, and there were the two sacks, but the big sack was so heavy that when Thursday came I had difficulty carrying it. I found the café, and no sooner had an old hakawati begun telling the love story of Antar and Abla but Omar walked in. He was wearing a white robe with a wonderful, black cloak and an embroidered silk vest, such as only the most elegant people in Damascus wore back then. He sat down next to me without a word of greeting, and when the hakawati had finished his tale, I stood up and started to leave, just as he had ordered. He grabbed me by my sleeve. 'What's in this sack?' he asked.

" 'Heavy hay,' I answered. He laughed, then

hoisted the sack and walked out. He climbed on his horse, which he had tied in front of the café, and rode alongside me. I walked slowly down the street.

" 'The police are bound to make a raid tonight. Where are you planning to spend the night?' he asked.

" 'I already have a hiding place for the next few years,' I answered.

" 'Yes, but where can I see you? Tell me where you'll be!' he whispered.

" 'O sir, two mountains will never meet, but two people will find each other if they look,' I answered.

" 'You have learned well. The time in prison was a fair price to pay for that. Keep your word, never let anyone leave your table hungry or dissatisfied!' he called out, then laughed and rode away under a mantle of darkness.

"And as for me, I came to your neighborhood and bought a dilapidated dump. The money allowed me to make it into the coffeehouse that all of you know. But I saw that the food was not enough to keep my guests satisfied. I saw how they would go back home with all their cares and worries. Then one night a guest happened to tell a beautiful story, and the people stayed longer and went home happier. From then on I hired a hakawati every night."

"My God, and did you ever meet Omar again?" Musa asked.

"No," answered Junis, but a smile played around his lips.

"You heard it," said Isam, "the master taught him
—he's never supposed to tell everything he knows."
Junis nodded, relieved. Isam pulled out five cards, and
just as on the previous evening, the
locksmith wanted to be the last
to draw. It was the emigrant
who drew the
ace.

8

*How
one person's
true story was not believed,
whereas his most blatant lie was*

Tuma the emigrant was a vigorous, wiry man of slight build. His gait was more a skip, despite the seventy-five years he carried on his back. He would bound up stairs as if he were a love-stricken fourteen-year-old on his way to see his sweetheart. None of the other gentlemen looked as young and strong as Tuma, whose entire philosophy of health consisted in taking an ice-cold shower every morning, in winter as well as summer. He always said he felt reborn after his shower.

Tuma came from a village on the coast, not far from Latakia. When he returned from America, not one member of his family was still living in the port city: some had died, and the rest had either moved to different cities or left the country. Tuma and his wife, Jeannette, decided to settle in Damascus. She was a second-generation emigrant, born in California; her mother came from Mexico. Her father, on the other hand, came from the mountains of Lebanon; an only child, he had lost his parents in the massacres of 1860. Sixty years later, shortly before his death, he made his only daughter swear never to return to Arabia, neither by land nor by sea. So when she did return, she insisted on a city with an airport, and Damascus did indeed boast an airport.

Tuma rented a very small house on Lazarists Street. If his wife Jeannette hadn't been so petite and thin, the two of them would never have been able to move at the same time inside the tiny rooms of their dollhouse. Nevertheless, in his forty square feet of courtyard Tuma was not to be deterred from constructing the pride and joy of every Arabian palace: what he had been raving to his wife about for thirty years—a fountain . . . in this case, no larger than a soup bowl. Surrounding this treasure was a miniature jungle of plants growing out of a thousand tiny flowerpots, which Tuma's clever hands had first fashioned from tin cans and then painted and arranged with such skill that the plants actually made the courtyard appear larger than it was. The only thing that bothered his friends was a plastic penguin, which spat water into the soup bowl in an uninterrupted noisy stream; if it hadn't come from America, then Salim, Mehdi, or Junis would have suggested to Tuma that he throw it in the trash. Or else Isam would have smashed the plastic bird into a thousand and one pieces. Faris and Musa, on the other hand, both agreed that the presence of the ice dweller in the middle of Damascus had a cooling effect on the soul.

Jeannette spoke a broken Arabic, but she said what

she thought directly and without the slightest embel-
lishment. Whenever he visited, Salim couldn't get
enough of her. He liked the freshness of her language.
The neighbors appreciated—and even envied—this
petite, gentle woman, for although she spoke so softly
she was nearly inaudible, she never had to repeat a
word she said. Jeannette had not been eager to leave
America, if for no other reason than it meant leaving
behind their grown-up children. But Tuma had
promised her heaven on earth if she came with him
to Syria: she would be his queen, he her slave. At least
that's how the neighbors told it. The strong-willed
Tuma was never in his life anybody's slave, but even
in public he showed his spouse great respect. He was
the only man in the neighborhood who walked hand
in hand with his wife.

Like many who returned from America, Tuma
dressed in a European suit and always wore one of the
many hats he had in his possession. They were as
beautiful as those worn by the gangster bosses in
American movies. And in the winter, when Tuma
wore his light-colored raincoat with the collar turned
up, Faris often greeted him with the words "Hello,
Mister Humphrey Bogart!"

That night, when Tuma walked in the room, his
friends were already waiting.

"I see that tonight Tuma's planning to entertain
our stomachs as well," Isam joked and made some
room on the small table for the tray of cookies Tuma

had brought along. Salim gave the emigrant a slightly disapproving eye: an Arab guest does not bring cookies. Tuma smiled, a little embarrassed. "In America," he said, "guests always bring something. Jeannette insisted. She sends you her greetings and says she's dying to know how you like her cookies. She made them according to an old Mexican recipe."

Salim smiled and took one; the others followed. "Now you can get away with any story you want," said Mehdi, laughing. "You've already bribed us."

"Okay, you all know I spent over thirty years in America, but none of you has ever asked why I went there in the first place." Tuma took a swallow of tea. "When the First World War broke out," the emigrant began his story, "I was eighteen years old."

"Eighteen!" Musa interrupted. "You were at least twenty-eight, my dear!"

"Let's call it twenty," the emigrant offered as a compromise.

Musa signaled his acceptance, and Tuma went on with his tale.

"We lived on the outskirts of Latakia. When the Ottoman military authorities called me up, I fled, but I had no idea where to go. Until that time, Latakia had been my whole world. My parents were very poor basket weavers. I had an uncle and an aunt who lived in Tartus, but I couldn't stay with them because their sons had also fled the draft and their houses were constantly being searched by the police.

"I wandered around the city and spent my nights by the sea with the poor fishermen. There were over twenty of us young men staying there. One day in the summer of 1916—I had been hiding there for two years—we woke up at dawn. A large detachment of soldiers was combing the coast, looking for people like me. Some informer had blown the whistle on us. I heard that for every man they caught he got one piaster! Anyone who ran was shot. I could see the soldiers' torches and could hear the cries of those they had captured.

"An Italian freighter was lying anchored off the coast; it had taken on tobacco in Latakia and was waiting for papers to put out to sea. I ran and ran, but the soldiers were closing in. There wasn't a single tree or bush for me to hide behind. I was so afraid, I found a high cliff and clambered up. One slip and you'd fall to your death. From my hideout I could see the flat beach off to my right. The soldiers were driving their quarry into the water and beating them with the butts of their rifles. Then they chained the prisoners together like unruly camels. I lay as flat as I could on the rock ledge. Soon it was light, and the soldiers kept on searching. They set fire to many of the fishermen's huts as a punishment. Even so, I thought my hiding place was safe until one of the soldiers with a pair of field glasses called out from the beach below: 'Bring that dog down here!' and three soldiers started climbing up to get me. My end was approaching—I could see it. The war was in back of me, and in front of me, the sea: two monsters! I didn't know how to swim. Funny, isn't it? We all lived by the sea, but most of my friends were every bit as scared of the water as I was."

"The proverb says: The cobbler goes barefoot, and the tailor is naked," said Faris.

Isam laughed. "You could also say: The fisherman drowns!"

"Okay," Tuma went on, "so the soldiers were cursing out loud as they climbed up to get me. Their clumsy boots kept slipping on the smooth rock. Their sergeant threatened to punish them if I escaped. When there was only about twenty feet left between us, I stood up. The soldiers gently tried to persuade me to spare them the danger. They said they were just poor devils too, who had no choice but to carry out their orders. I took one step in their direction, but then I cried out and jumped into the ocean. I had no idea how high the cliff really was.

"When I hit the water, I started thrashing my arms furiously. All I could hear or see was water. The freighter wasn't far off but the sea kept pulling me down. I struggled like a crazy man. I no longer remember how long I kept going. I just kept shouting, 'I want to live!' and flailed about and flailed about until I had exhausted all my strength. When I came to, I found myself surrounded by friendly faces. I jumped up and wanted to run away, but the sailors calmed me down. They had watched the whole search action, and when they saw me jump, they secretly let down a boat. As long as the ship was anchored their captain had to be kept in the dark, otherwise he'd get into trouble and have to hand me over to the authorities. But the next day the ship set sail for Venice.

"Okay, so in Venice I was able to find work as a porter. There were many Arabs working there. But I wanted to go to America. A cousin of mine lived in Florida. At the time I thought: Well, why not? I'll find him. America's big, sure, but it can't be much bigger than Latakia—and in Latakia you can mention a man's name and before the day is over you've found him." Tuma laughed, took a draw on the waterpipe, and passed it to Salim. Then he went on.

"My word, was America bigger than Latakia! I've often told you what hell the immigration authorities put us through. Okay, so it turned out that in the meantime my cousin had moved on to Argentina looking for work. Argentina means 'land of silver,' and my cousin hoped he'd find some in a country that size. You know, when an emigrant needs something to hold on to, a spider web looks like a wooden beam. None of you have ever emigrated, but let me tell you, it's a hard life. Bread was like a horseman, and we emigrants were always racing after him on foot with our tongues hanging out, huffing and puffing, trying to catch up with him. A curse, I can tell you.

"Okay. You've told some fantastic stories. But I

experienced so much in America that I won't have to tell you anything but the truth. It often hurts me that so many people here think there's money lying in the street over there. They say that in America things are different: you just bend down and you can pick dollar bills more easily than tomatoes in the fields outside Damascus. And if you tell these people it isn't true, maybe they won't tell you to your face that you're an idiot, no no, but they'll make you feel like one. Look at this man, or look at that one, they say. He spent two years in America and came back a millionaire! It hurts to see the contempt in people's eyes. A neighbor once told me when he was drunk: 'Anyone who makes it in America doesn't come back.' Let me tell you, that may be the case for a lot of people, but not for me. The older I got, the more homesick I became for my Latakia. I never felt any kind of longing for homeland, or fatherland, or any other bullshit—but I had to go back to Latakia. It's like you have to take revenge for the disgrace of running away. You go back to prove yourself as a human being, to show you're stronger than war, stronger than hunger, or stronger than the sea. Meanwhile here they're waiting for you with the question: 'Come on, Mr. America, why don't you buy yourself a villa?' No one asks: 'What did you get out of being abroad?' Last night I thought for a long time about what being abroad had given me, and what it had taken away. That's what I

want to tell you about tonight. So please listen as if it were a story. Okay?

"I did get rich living abroad, but not so much with money as with a second life. I think there was one Tuma who died when he jumped into the ocean and another Tuma who was born on board that boat. In my first life I used to be scared of my own shadow, but when I walked off the deck of that ship I went into the New World like a lion. What more did I have to lose? From then on, the greatest danger was no worse than the cackling of a hen. So, being abroad gave me a courage I had never known.

"Also, in Latakia we lived like bees—the individual didn't count, the clan was everything. It gives you a feeling of security, but it also ties your hands and feet up. In America people live like gazelles, everyone for himself, even if they travel together. You're on your own, but you're also free to try something new. Over there you get in a boat and row across the river all by yourself. Here if you want to cross the river to some new shore you have to pack everyone in the boat first: two grandfathers and two grandmothers, your father and mother, brothers and sisters, aunts and uncles, not to mention all the in-laws."

"You're forgetting preacher and imam," Faris added, nodding his head in agreement.

"If I can't take along our waterpipe and our Arabian mocha as well," Isam added with a serious ex-

141

Leabharlanna Poiblí Chathair Bhaile Átha Cliath

Dublin City Public Libraries

pression, "I couldn't care less about any new shores."

"Okay, that's not a bad idea, but unfortunately it's impossible. But let me get back to America! In Latakia I might have met a few foreigners working on the boats, but in America I lived with Greeks, Chinese, Africans, Poles, Jews, Italians, and you name it —from any country in the world. There you meet people who had lived completely different lives before. And not just poor devils, either. You meet distinguished people working on the docks right next to you—people who'd never lifted a thing in their life. I even met Kahlil Gibran."

"You mean the famous poet Gibran?" Faris asked incredulously.

"Yes, Gibran. We were both living in New York. I met him in 1921 at a reading. He was a good man whose language and voice just streamed into my heart the first moment I heard him and filled it with peace. But while he was still alive there were many jealous people who attacked him and tried to smear his reputation. They wouldn't even leave his private life alone. But what harm can a fly's shit do to an elephant? And in his soul Gibran was as big as an elephant. One day we were in a small bar. He was very sad and he asked me how he should defend himself against his enemies. They wouldn't give him a single day of peace. Imagine, the great scholar Gibran asking me, a simple dockhand, what he should do. I told him to do just what my grandfather had done: my grandfather confounded his enemies because he kept going straight ahead.

"I bought all of Kahlil's books and had him write a fine dedication. 'To my friends Jeannette and Tuma,' he wrote. My wife loved him as much as I did. When he died of cancer in 1931, many Arabs and Americans mourned his passing. To this day my wife shows the books to every guest, and I agree with her when she says they're the greatest treasure we have.

"Okay, so what did I get out of living abroad and what did I lose? You know, before I went to America, I used to love to talk. I can still remember how I lost two jobs in Latakia because I talked and sang too much. I didn't know what a word was really worth until I traveled abroad and lost my voice. Words are invisible jewels; the only people who can see them are the ones who've lost them. Salim knows this better than anyone."

The old coachman nodded pensively.

"But losing your voice in a foreign country is worse than never having had one. Salim understands exactly what I mean. It's a particularly bitter form of dumbness, for those who are born dumb can speak with their hands, their eyes, their head. In fact, they speak with everything but their tongue. But we foreigners have it as bad as the hero of Mehdi's story. What was his name again? Shafik?"

"No, Shafak," Mehdi corrected.

"At first everything is dead, just like with Shafak.

I hadn't learned to talk with my hands any more than Salim. Then suddenly I was in America. But I stayed voiceless for a long time, even after I could speak English."

"Why was that?" Mehdi wanted to know.

"How are you going to talk to people who don't have the faintest idea about the things that really matter to you? I went to America with the heart of a lion and the patience of a camel, but courage and patience were no cure for being mute. Being abroad gave me the tongue of a child, and soon it gave me a child's heart to match. You know that heart and tongue are made from the same flesh. And I spoke with the heart and tongue of a child and the patience of a camel. But no matter what I told them, they treated everything I said as a fairy tale. The Americans have a huge country, but they know very little about the rest of the world. They called me a Turk, even though I explained a thousand times that Syria is a separate country, that it only borders on Turkey. What's the difference, most of them said, you're all Turks. On the other hand, they insisted that I know exactly where *they* came from, down to the side of the street where they were born. In New York, bitter foes sometimes live jammed right next to one another, and woe unto you if you confuse one side of the street in Harlem with another. Or try to explain to an American that you're both an Arab *and* a Christian. They'd find it easier to swallow Aladdin's lamp.

"Once I was taking the train on my way to visit a friend named Mahmoud el-Haj. He was an engineer at an electrical appliance plant."

"El-Haj from Malula?"

"No, Mahmoud came from southern Lebanon. Okay, so the trip takes thirty hours by train. At one point this American comes into my compartment. He gives me a friendly nod, and I'm looking forward to a conversation that will make the trip a little shorter. But that was too much to hope for. 'Are you a Turk?' he asked.

" 'No,' I said, 'I'm an Arab.'

" 'That doesn't matter, as long as you're a Muslim. I've recently converted to Islam. Ashhadu anna la ilaha illa Allahu wa anna Muhammadan Rasulu Allah.' The American recited the words of his creed to me, but that one sentence was all the Arabic he knew.

" 'Okay, that's fine for you, but I'm not a Muslim. I'm Christian, you know?'

" 'Hmm,' he says. The young American was confused and thought for a long time. Then he gave me a disapproving look. 'So you're not really an Arab, you're a Mexican!'

" 'No, I'm not, I'm as Arab as they come. There's a poet in every generation of my family.'

" 'Hmm,' he said again, sighing, and was again silent for a long time. 'But if you're an Arab, then you have to be a Muslim, that is for sure!'

" 'No, nothing is for sure. In Arabia there are Jews,

Christians, Muslims, Druses, Baha'is, Yezidis, and many other religious groups besides.'

" 'Hmm,' he repeated and looked at me. By now he was completely unnerved. 'No, all Arabs are Muslims. After all, they're the ones who invented Islam!' He was very disappointed, as if the Arabs had left him in the lurch with his Islam."

"Are Americans stupid, or was this man's deck just missing a few cards?" Isam wanted to know.

"No. You know, Americans are no more stupid and no more smart than Arabs. You won't believe it when I tell you about the skyscrapers in New York!"

"And why not? I've seen pictures in the paper!" Junis said reassuringly.

"Okay, but I'm positive you won't believe me when I tell you that Americans don't haggle when they buy things!"

"What do they do, swat flies?" Isam sounded indignant.

"No, but when you go into a store, you just look at the price tags, you pay, and leave."

"Now you're making fun of us," Isam objected.

"No, I didn't believe it at first, either, but after I had learned the language, I went into a big store, six stories high. You could find everything you wanted: clothes, food, toys, material, paint, radios."

"So it was a bazaar. All in one building?" Musa asked amazed.

"That's right, a bazaar all in one building, except

you can't haggle. I can tell you don't believe me, even the eyes of my dear friend Salim are accusing me of lying."

Salim felt he had been caught and smiled.

"Okay, so I went in. I wanted to buy a jacket. I found one I liked and took it to a saleslady. 'How much does this jacket cost?' I asked.

"The woman looked at me in astonishment. 'You can read it right there, mister. It's written on the tag: fifty dollars,' she said in a friendly way.

" 'That's very true, that's what's written on the tag, but life is a conversation, dear lady—question and answer, give and take! I'll pay twenty,' I told her, like anyone here would start the bargaining.

" 'Give and take? Question and answer?' She was so bewildered she was stammering. But then she calmed down and started speaking very loudly; she must have thought I was hard of hearing: *Jacket costs fifty. Half of one-hundred-dollar bill!'* And to make things absolutely clear, she pointed to the price on the tag again.

" 'Is that your last word? All right, I'll pay twenty-five, so you can say you've made a good deal.'

" 'What do you mean, last word? Twenty-five? It says fifty. Can't you read? *Five-oh!'* the lady screamed and wrote the number fifty on some wrapping paper next to the register.

" 'Okay, okay, I don't want to disappoint a charming young lady like you, and have you think I'm stingy or something. I'll pay thirty,' I told her, because I wanted to help her. 'I'm a new customer here, and if we can reach an agreement today, then I'll be a regular from now on,' I added—words guaranteed to break the last resistance of any dealer in Damascus.

"But now this woman was completely flabbergasted. 'A regular? What are you talking about? Listen, mister, I'm just doing my job here. The jacket costs fifty bucks. Take it or leave it,' she snapped impatiently.

"That made me mad. But I heeded the advice I once heard from my father: 'If the seller's so dumb he doesn't come down on the price, then raise your offer a little and say you're going. If he's so dumb he still doesn't get the idea, then just walk out slowly and don't look back. Don't let him know you're attached to the thing. That's written in the Bible: Thou shalt not turn around! Then he's bound to call after you and lower the price a little.' My poor father, he never saw America! So I raised my offer to forty dollars and told the woman, 'If you're not interested in doing business today, I'll go to someone else and buy the same jacket for twenty dollars.' I laid the jacket down and walked out slowly, without turning around. Any seller in Latakia or Damascus would have called after me and tried to save the deal, but she didn't say a word. In thirty years not a single person ever called after me. I gave up trying to haggle."

"There's no way on earth I could live in America," Isam moaned.

"You're also not going to believe me when I tell you that the Americans keep their cemeteries clean and tidy and even decorate them. Whenever it's sunny they go walking in the cemetery."

"Oh, come on, now you've really broken your promise about telling us the truth—these are plain fairy tales! Walking in the cemetery?" Junis was indignant, and the others shook their heads as if they felt sorry for the emigrant. Ali was just putting a large piece of wood in the stove when he heard the word *cemetery*. "May God protect us from all harm!" he prayed. Only Faris knew from his student days in Paris that Tuma wasn't lying, but the former statesman preferred to keep silent and let Tuma endure the wrath of the others all on his own.

Salim thought the emigrant was lying, but he just smiled at how desperate Tuma must be if he wanted to pass this lie off as truth.

"I swear by Saint—" Tuma began, to lend some support to his statement about walking in the cemetery.

"For heaven's sake, don't swear!" Junis yelled at him. "We don't want anything to happen to you."

"Oh my God," Tuma moaned in despair while the others laughed out loud.

"A graveyard is a place of ruin," said Junis, fuming,

"and not a place of pleasure. Just look at our cemeteries! In time they decay, just like the bones they shelter under the earth. Earth to earth, say the Holy Scriptures, and not earth to pleasure palace. What crazy soul would build a cemetery to last? Any Arab would sooner forget about death today than tomorrow!"

"The Americans, too, but in a different way," Tuma shouted back. "They act as if death didn't matter to them, and they go walking in its place as if they'd completely forgotten about it."

"I'm only going there once," said Musa, frowning on the heated quarrel. "Have you heard the story about the test of courage that was held in a cemetery?"

"Which one?" asked Isam, who knew a number of similar stories, which in Damascus were mostly told on cold winter nights.

"The one with the chicken!"

"No, I don't know any with a chicken. Please, go on and tell it! Maybe you'll inspire Tuma," Isam requested and patted the emigrant on the shoulder.

"There once was a bet," Musa began, "where the winner would be the one who could go to a fresh grave at dusk and calmly eat a chicken stuffed with rice, raisins, and pine nuts. The challenger accused a whole village of being cowards and offered a large sack of money as a reward for the hero who came back with the bare chicken bones. All the respected men in the village lost the bet, for those who actually managed to sit down in the graveyard lost their courage when a pale hand came out of the earth and grabbed at the food and a voice roared from the grave, 'Let us have a taste!' Naturally no one knew that an accomplice of the challenger had hidden himself beforehand in the empty grave.

"One day a poor half-starved, emaciated devil came forward. The villagers split their sides laughing when he asked, 'Is the chicken fresh?'

" 'Yes,' they told him, 'a fresh chicken is prepared every time.'

"So the man went without the slightest hesitation to the designated grave. Then he sat down, tore the chicken in two, and started devouring it. When the hand came out of the earth and the voice roared, the man just turned away and shouted back, 'First the living have to have their fill, then the dead can have their due!' But the hand grabbed at the chicken once again. So the man jumped up and began stomping on the hand until the accomplice in the grave begged for mercy.

"The man walked back to the village with the bare bones. People hoisted him up on their shoulders, and the village elder held a great speech in his honor. But the man just kept burping and complaining, 'The chicken wasn't fresh at all.' "

Tuma laughed. "Well, you are incorrigible, but in any case, the Americans live differently—and they didn't believe me any more than you do when I told them about how we live. They, too, accused me of telling fairy tales. They couldn't believe that we really ride camels and eat figs, or that we celebrate weddings for days and days and mourn the dead for even longer, but never celebrate our birthdays."

"Why should anyone celebrate his birthday?" Isam interrupted. "And, besides, if you know your own birthday you'll just get older and older. I, on the other hand, feel twenty years younger today than I did ten years ago."

"But for the Americans a birthday is more important than Easter," Tuma again picked up the thread. "And they'll celebrate a birthday on the fourth floor despite the fact that a neighbor's just died on the third. They didn't believe me when I told them we have professional storytellers in our cafés. All they did was laugh at me. And they didn't even want to hear about the steam bath."

"What's the matter with them," wondered Ali, "are they barbarians?"

"No, but people don't believe what's new to them, and any miracle becomes what the Americans call 'old hat' if it lasts a couple days. And now you're not going to believe me when I tell you that the Americans treat dogs better than they treat human beings."

"Look, why don't you just go on and tell us a real fairy tale instead of feeding us these lies about the

Americans. I'm only putting up with them because your cookies are so good," Junis gibed.

"No, what he says about the dogs is true, I know that from France," said the minister, at whom Tuma had glanced imploringly. "The French don't really treat their dogs better than people, but they do pamper the little mongrels!"

But Faris' defense of Tuma only poured oil on the fire, and soon Salim began clapping his hands and laughing.

"Don't try to confuse the issue with all your talk of France and America," said Junis. "Next you're going to say that dogs are waited on in restaurants. 'What will you have, Mr. Dog, for your entrée? Today I especially recommend my right thigh with thyme and tomato sauce!' " The men all laughed, and Salim threw himself onto his bed and gripped his stomach. Tears were streaming down his red cheeks.

"No one said anything about a restaurant!" said Tuma, annoyed. "But, in America, dogs do have over twenty brands of food!"

"I trust they have barbers as well?" Musa taunted.

"No," Tuma lied, and hated himself for doing it; on his way to Salim's he had solemnly undertaken to tell only what he had personally experienced in America—and now he had broken his oath. For years he had been longing to open his heart to his friends.

He had known it would be difficult, but he never imagined the old men would resist so fiercely.

"What about a dog cemetery?" Ali suddenly wanted to know.

"No, no," Tuma lied, out of exhaustion and desperation. He looked at the faces around him and thought how lucky Moses, Jesus, and Mohammed really were, not to have had such companions. Now he determined simply to lie to them. "Okay," he said and sighed with relief, "I still wanted to tell you about this one unusual man. I worked for him as a bookkeeper for ten years. As a young man he'd been very poor, but he was a sly devil and completely without scruples. The wars had made him rich, and he traded in anything that could be bought and sold. He wasn't exactly a miser, but he didn't put much stock in idle talk. Whenever you mentioned someone, he'd ask, 'What does he sell?' And if you told him the man didn't sell anything but was a very important person, he'd ask, 'What's his price?' You couldn't tell this moneybags a thing without his asking for the price.

"Okay, so during our lunch break we used to sit in the yard and swap stories about our countries. But all he ever did was laugh at us. 'You'll never get anywhere that way. Buying and selling—that's all a man needs to know,' he scoffed.

"One day an immigrant from Crete asked to hear an authentic Arabian love story. This man was like our Salim. He loved stories more than anything else.

I wanted to tell him the story of Kais and Leila, but he knew that one—also the one about Antar and Abla. He had heard them before, from other Arabs. Okay, so I told him about the sad fate of a young woman who hadn't wanted to marry her cousin because she was in love with the village smith. My grandfather had told me the story a long time ago. In fact, he had lived it, because he was the village smith.

"So the workers listened, and one or two of them cried, even though they had never been in Arabia. But Mr. Wilson—that was the man's name—just stood by the door, pretending to be engrossed in his stock reports. After I'd finished, he laughed himself silly over my heroes' sufferings and sorrows. 'My dear Thomas'—that's how they say Tuma in English— 'what's the point of this idiotic story?' Then he went on with what was for him a very detailed explanation: 'All the happiness that's taken you hours to describe in your story I can buy in five minutes: I can buy your beautiful woman—and the Arabian horse to boot. For a few dollars I could have someone kill the stubborn father of the bride who refused to give his consent. What's the big deal? You don't need a story for all that, just plain hard work.'

" 'Mister, there's a lot of things that nobody on earth can buy,' I answered bitterly, since he had made light of my grandmother's suffering and her courage.

"He laughed. 'Such as what?'

" 'Such as a single moment of happiness, even one

as fleeting as the wind,' I answered and walked out. I could still hear his laughter ringing out behind me.

" 'You can buy wind, too, my dear Thomas! My portable fan costs ten dollars and fifty cents,' he roared whenever he saw me over the next weeks.

"Well, Mr. Wilson was successful. Stock reports and news about wars and droughts were all that interested him; he detested stories. And so the years passed. One day his wife suddenly left him. He was absolutely miserable; nothing could change her mind, neither threats nor money. Mr. Wilson was so unhappy he completely lost his will to live. For days he wouldn't eat. He just hung about the office, dead to the world. He refused to wash or shave. After three days we informed a close business associate of his—he had no other friends. Well, this Mr. Eden was a man of the world and he happened to like Wilson. He hurried to see him and took him to some island for a vacation. Okay, so Mr. Wilson was already over fifty, and as much as he liked to boast about buying happiness, he was basically an unhappy man who had never found any peace.

"Well, he went with his friend and stayed away for a month. When he came back, he was suntanned and happy. Following his friend's advice, he resolved from then on to enjoy a leisurely breakfast every morning, to swim for at least an hour every afternoon, to have a long massage every day, and every evening to take a young woman to a restaurant and the theater, or to the movies. In the office he started reading all the New York tabloids. We brought him every bit of rubbish that was printed on paper. He read the colorful pages and laughed.

"One day he read that the costliest thing in life was time. It was worth more than gold and jewels. Mr. Wilson remembered me and had me sent for. 'You're right, my dear Thomas, time is worth more than gold. It says so right here!' He showed me the picture of a healer whose hands had the power to prolong life by years. The healer was supposedly one hundred fifty years old. But his face was as smooth as an eighteen-year-old's. Mr. Wilson's eyes grew bright when he told me everything he now intended to catch up on. So he went to this healer and paid a large amount of money to have his life prolonged by one year. From then on, Mr. Wilson lived very happily. Whether just by a fluke or not, the very next day he fell in love with a young woman who brought him even more happiness. But no more than nine months had passed when he called me in a second time. Again he looked worried. He was concerned he might die too soon, now that he had tasted happiness. He tried to persuade the healer to sell him twenty years, but the healer refused. He could only sell time by the month, as he had so many customers waiting in line.

"A few days later, Mr. Wilson again appeared somewhat relieved. He had gone to great effort and spent a huge amount of money to buy two and a half months from the healer. The miracle man assured him that only Henry Ford could buy more than that.

"Well, the months of happiness passed quickly and made Mr. Wilson's lust for time even greater. Two days before the time he'd bought ran out, he caught pneumonia. But he refused to go to the doctor. Instead he sent for the man with the miraculous hands, but it turned out that the old healer had died the week before.

"Mr. Wilson's secretary raced back to him in the hope of convincing him to send for the doctor after all. But when Mr. Wilson heard the news, he cried out like a wounded animal. He died the very next day."

Tuma looked at the pale faces of his listeners, and a smile curled briefly around his mouth.

"Now that's a story!" Junis raved, "My friend, you really have seen the world!"

"It's true," said Musa. "Nobody could make up a story like that. You have to experience it!"

"The great Napoleon knew what he was talking about when he said a man must spend three years abroad before he really becomes a man," Faris added.

"That was easy for Napoleon to say," Tuma answered drily. "I'm sure he didn't say it in New York Harbor or on the Hudson River on some rainy day so cold you curse the hour you were born."

The friends went on talking about time and happiness late into the night, but Tuma didn't hear a word.

He was mulling over his disappointment, over the fact that the others had not only accepted this lie as plain truth, they had even praised it—whereas all he had done was cobble together a story from a small announcement in the *New York Times* and the names of presidents and prime ministers.

Shortly after twelve, Isam started to lay out the cards, but the old barber tapped him on the shoulder. "Leave it, my friend. After such a wonderful story, I'm craving to tell one myself. I will volunteer to be the ace tomorrow, if no one minds." The minister and Isam didn't mind. And Ali the locksmith? He was so relieved he whooped for joy: "Wonderful!"

9

How
a certain man
mastered all the lies in the world
but missed the one truth right in front of his nose

If in the late 1950s you had asked for Musa the barber, anyone in the old town would have been sure to ask right back: "Do you mean the Musa who raises doves or Musa the miser?" And since Salim's friend did not possess a single dove, it was easy to guess how bad Musa's reputation really was in the old quarter. But like so many reputations, this one, too, was unjust: the slanderers of Damascus failed to distinguish between carefully hidden poverty and true stinginess. And the truth was that Musa was poor; in fact, very poor, and he had a large family to feed. A half-hour battle with the wildest bush of hair earned him no more than half a lira, while for a shave he received a pitiful quarter-lira. He had to shear through a full hour's worth of hair to earn three quarters of a lira. After that, Musa was exhausted, but he was nonetheless happy when the next customer arrived to keep the barber's chair warm. Each day, every day (except on Monday) Musa plowed through ten hours of hair; even so, the money he earned was barely enough to stave hunger from his door.

Of course, it was difficult to tell whether any barber in Damascus was truly poor. The white smock, the freshly shaven face, the neatly oiled hair, and the constant fragrance of cologne made every barber shine like a well-to-do gentleman. If he were also on the plump side, as was Musa, then no power on earth could persuade Damascenes that he was poor. In Arabia to be fat meant you were rich. Of course, there's nothing surprising about that, since the majority of Arabs hardly ever had anything to eat and always led such a hard life beneath the scorching sun that it was almost impossible to find a single gram of unnecessary fat on their bones. The only people who actually did grow plump were those who lived lives of comfort in the palaces. Film stars and belly dancers followed this aristocratic tradition, keeping themselves royally stuffed so that they, too, would radiate health and prosperity.

Not only was Musa a bit portly; he also kept his hair oiled and dyed and parted crisply down the middle; and his smile revealed two rows of pearly white teeth that were visible from a great distance, so that his overall appearance was that of a well-nourished film star. Who could possibly believe that this barber began every morning by dividing up his customers? The first three for the rent, the next two for vegetables. One customer for salt, sugar, and tea, and two more had to provide for the children's clothing and medication. If another client showed up, Musa's fam-

ily might have a little meat. When the barber was especially lucky and a generous gentleman tipped him an extra quarter-lira, Musa would immediately spend it on fruit, which he would carry home that very same day, happy and proud.

As mentioned, Musa never skimped on oil and dye for his hair. People in the old quarter muttered rumors about his seducing young girls, but that was an exaggeration. Only once in his life, over forty years ago, had he seduced a young woman, and that was the one he married.

Every day Musa gave the flower vendor, Nuri, a special shave—in exchange for a red carnation, which he wore in his buttonhole. Musa's boutonniere confused his poor neighbors even more, since the only people who wore carnations in their buttonholes were Farid el-Atrash, the famous singer, who came from a noble family, and the millionaire George Sehnaui.

This evening everyone was anxiously awaiting the barber's tale. It was understood throughout the old town that he was a terrible barber but a great storyteller, and his customers put up with a bad haircut and one or two nicks in order to listen to him talk, or else to tell him their secrets, for Musa was a deep well indeed.

When Musa walked into the coachman's room, Salim and his friends wondered for a moment at the old brown leather bag the barber was carrying, but

then went right back to their quarrel. "Wherever you go, people tell you, 'Shhh, the walls have ears,' and ever since the walls grew these ears, we've lost our tongues." Junis was shouting at the minister.

"But what does that have to do with the transistor radio?" Faris angrily wanted to know.

"I don't know, but the whole damned thing began with this miserable transistor . . ." Junis groaned.

"That's my impression as well," confirmed the teacher. "Before, people used to argue with one another, as equals among equals. Nowadays transistor radios have descended on the country like a swarm of locusts. There's one in every room, even if there isn't any electricity. The government can reach you in the remotest steppe to proclaim the one and only valid truth. There's nothing that separates the government from its subjects anymore. The president and his cronies whisper and shout their opinions right into our ears, as if they were old friends. Isn't that right? Back when you were in office, my dear Faris, you and your colleagues were pretty bad off without this portable radio. But now, just look at Nasser. He can reach anybody. He can even tell jokes to the man on the street. That's right, jokes: 'Go on and laugh, my friend,' says Nasser. 'Have you heard the one about price hikes?' Oh Nasser's good, all right—there's never been anyone better, at least not when it comes to making an ass of the entire population."

"Would you please let Musa tell his story!" interrupted Faris.

Ali and Salim nodded their heads in clear support of the minister's suggestion.

"So, may I finally begin? After all, tonight is my night, is it not?" Musa asserted unambiguously. "I have a feeling," he said as Salim handed him the tea glass, "that the face muscles loosen up when they're soaped, and that's why my clients tell me things they wouldn't even trust to their wives or confessors. But a lot of what they say is boring, and you need the patience of Job to sift through it all and find a plum.

"Of course," Musa went on, "all of us are pretty bad listeners, since Salim has spoiled us with the best stories around. Anyone can listen to an exciting story; but a good listener is like a determined gold prospector patiently digging through the mud to find a little nugget of the prized metal. But enough talk about listening, now I want to say something about telling. When I began my apprenticeship, my master told me: 'A barber tells a client whatever he wants to hear.' In my opinion that's good advice for bad barbers. I've always told only what I wanted to tell. Under my shears every head was equal, whether it belonged to a judge or just any poor devil. I was never afraid to talk; after all, it was me holding the razor, not the customer.

"So. Tonight I want to tell you a little story about lies, since I know my friend Salim loves lies. And if it

doesn't bother you, I'd like to cut my friend's hair at the same time. One snip of the scissors and one word, a stroke of the comb and a sentence—that way I feel better, and besides, Salim hasn't had his hair cut in ages."

Salim rolled his eyes, as if he preferred to stay mute rather than subject himself to the barber's blades and scissors.

"Don't be afraid, Salim," Ali consoled. "I'll be sitting across from you, and if Musa nicks you, just close your eyes and I'll whack him one that'll have him hanging on the wall next to the portrait of your wife."

The others all laughed, and this heartened Salim. Junis spread a newspaper under the chair so that the clippings wouldn't fall on the small carpet, and the old coachman took his seat in the middle of the room.

Musa opened his leather bag. With one swing he put on his snow-white smock, then covered Salim with a brownish barber's wrap. Next he carefully arranged his shears, brushes, and an old electric cutter on a cloth he had spread out on the bed. Musa hadn't felt this good in a long time. He clicked his Solingen shears in the air a few times, gathered a clump of the coachman's hair with his comb, and snipped it off in a single swipe.

"So . . . they say Damascus has had more rulers than its buildings have stones—although the smallest heap of mortar and the tiniest of stones live longer than any human being." Musa grabbed a second bunch of hair, but as he did so he ran his comb right into the coachman's scalp.

"Watch out!" called Ali.

"Salim's still counting on a long life ahead of him!" Isam reminded the barber.

"My hands aren't what they used to be," Musa continued, paying careful attention to the next cut. "Anyhow, as I was saying, more rulers than stones. And very few of these rulers actually died in their beds, though the king I want to tell you about today had lived a long life, and now he was lying on his deathbed. When death began to quietly stroke his feet, the king sent for his only son, Prince Sadek, who came and sat beside the royal bed. In a quiet voice, the king asked his ministers and servants to leave the royal chamber so that he could be alone with his son."

Salim winced when he felt another stab behind his ear, and his hand jerked up. But this time Ali didn't notice because he was putting a log into the stove.

Isam laughed. "Now listen, Musa, just because Ali isn't watching doesn't mean you can butcher our Salim!"

The barber went on cutting and then snapped his scissors for show. "Oh, that's all part of the haircut. His hair's just shaggy. It pulls a little." Nevertheless, he wetted some gauze with a little cologne and dabbed it on the wound.

"So, alone with his son, right. 'My son,' said the king, 'soon I will leave this world and knock at the

door that opens but once. You are inheriting a mighty kingdom. Show mercy to your friends when they eat at your table, and to your foes when they fall into your hands. Be a friend to highwaymen and smugglers, but protect yourself from liars. They will be your slow death.' Thus spoke the king and his soul expired.

" 'The king is dead! Long live the king!' the messengers cried out across the land.

"So, King Sadek hadn't yet turned eighteen the day he ascended the throne. He was merciless with friend and foe. In less than a year Damascus had become a city of misery. His people were going hungry, but that didn't bother King Sadek. Instead, he announced his resolve to learn every lie in the world. From early in the morning until late at night he listened to the master liars recite all the lies known to date, whether about foxes, humans, demons, or elves. For thirty years the king worked diligently to learn the lies of Arabs, Jews, Hindus, Greeks, and Chinese. For thirty years he paid out generous sums until he had mastered a thousand and one lies. When he began the thirty-first year of his reign, the king proclaimed: 'No man on earth can tell me a new lie!'

" 'Come, now!' the court fool disagreed. 'Lies and locusts are cousins. Every new person born into the world is accompanied by seven lies and seven locusts. And no one can live long enough to count all those lies and locusts,' he explained."

"A wise man, this fool," said Faris. "From what I can tell, our whole government consists exclusively of lying locusts." Salim laughed so hard he shook, and if Musa hadn't been paying attention, he would have inflicted a second wound upon the old coachman. Ali, too, roared with laughter.

"You better quiet down," Junis warned. "Yesterday they took away the son of Um Khalil, the midwife, for talking about a banana."

"A banana?" Musa wondered.

"He happened to be holding a straight, green banana. It was small and strange-looking; the devil only knows where he found a banana like that. He was drunk and said out loud, 'I know why it's so hard to find bananas these days. It's because they're all being forced to follow the government line, the crooked creatures. Take this one here. It still smells like a banana, but see, it's already beginning to look like a cucumber!' He was standing in front of my son's bar, babbling out loud and laughing. Some neighbors tried to pull him inside, but before they could, two men from the secret police showed up. They beat him and took him away."

"Miserable scoundrels," sighed Tuma.

"So . . . where was I?" asked Musa, and without waiting for an answer, he went on: "So . . . right. King Sadek thought he had heard all the lies on earth and nothing in the world could surprise him; the

court fool said that lies and locusts were cousins; no man on earth could count them. So . . . that's where I left off.

" 'All right,' the king commanded his fool, 'have it proclaimed that I will reward anyone who tells me a new lie with his weight in gold. But if he should fail, then off with his head!'

"No sooner said than done! Faster than the wind, the news traveled all the way to India and China, and the liars and soothsayers all hurried to get their fill of gold. But no matter what they said, they couldn't surprise the king."

"He was lucky he didn't know our government— they would have taken every last piece of gold he owned. Their lies do have a precise beginning, but no end," Faris commented caustically.

"For heaven's sake, let Musa tell his story!" Tuma interrupted.

"As I was saying," the barber continued, "the liars and soothsayers of all lands came flocking to Damascus, full of hope. But whatever lie they told, whether it was about a cow slipping out of an egg or about cities where melons grew as big as camels, the king would stifle a yawn and answer: 'What's new about that? That's lie number thirteen!' or 'That's lie number seven hundred and two!'

"Each liar was granted only one hour; the king wouldn't listen any longer. The minute the last grain

of sand tumbled through the straits of the hourglass, he waved his hand and delivered the liar to the executioner.

"This news, too, spread quickly throughout the world, with the result that many liars and soothsayers turned back when they heard what kind of lies the king considered commonplace, and that the tellers were all leaving a head shorter than they arrived. Not one of the poor souls got so much as a glimpse of any gold.

"After a few years, no one dared any longer to tell the king a lie, not even his ministers or his wife. Soon King Sadek was sitting proudly on his throne and laughing at the fool. 'You see, the door is open, but no one is coming. Where are all your locusts?'

" 'Your Majesty evidently knows every lie there is to know,' groveled the fool.

"At precisely that moment, an emaciated man dressed in rags appeared in the hall. All the guests, ministers, princes, and advisors roared with laughter until the king raised his hand. 'Speak, stranger!' he commanded.

" 'Salaam aleikum is what anyone who speaks should first say, and then, let come what will,' said the man without the slightest fear.

" 'Aleikum salaam,' replied the king. 'And now, stranger, your sand has begun to run,' the king added, turning over the hourglass.

" 'I am hungry. I haven't had anything to eat or

drink but water for over a week, and when my stomach's empty my head can't give birth to any lies—all it can do is conjure up thoughts of the most delicious dishes in the world,' the man declared, and as if he had told a joke, the king laughed.

" 'I can tell already that if you go on like this you will soon be relieved of your head entirely,' he said for the merriment of his guests and ordered a richly laden table to be set for the man.

" 'First I would like to enjoy my meal, then I will win the wager against Your Eminence—and in short order, too. But may I, O prince of the faithful, call my wife to join me? She, too, has gone without food for a week and a day, since she gave her last meal to me,' the man spoke quietly.

"The king was amused by the man's courage and granted his request. A small woman stepped forward. She was thinner than a shadow. Without a word she sat down beside her husband and both proceeded to eat very slowly.

" 'O mighty king, I thank you for this meal the likes of which even the emperor of China never saw. You should know that Chinese is one of my hundred languages. I can speak with people and animals. In fact a jackass can understand me better than you, O ruler of the faithful.'

" 'Impudent liar!' many of the guests called out, but the king just smiled. 'Speaking with jackasses: lie number thirty-five. If you go on boring me like that,

you'll be speaking with fish in less than half an hour.'

" 'Have patience, O king,' the man continued, un-daunted, 'everything in its time, for the spring unfolds its beauty with such magic only because it is preceded by the winter. So, when I first left our land, I served with the emperor of China. During that time he waged many wars. In one of these wars he was hit by three thousand arrows. But the arrows couldn't harm him, because I had rubbed him with ant's milk. I used to milk my ants each morning. But the ant's milk couldn't save him from the banana peel. He slipped and fell and was dead on the spot. The Chinese ban-ished me, and so my wife and I wandered the earth with only hunger for a companion. I grew so thin the wind sang songs between my ribs. When the angel of death heard the melody of my bones, his desire awak-ened for my soul. He came to fetch it. But he had to search for me a long time, since I was so thin I no longer had a shadow. I wanted to live, but the angel of death didn't want to go back empty-handed, so we fought each other fiercely—he with his scythe and I with my love of life. We fought for three hours until I killed him.'

" 'Unheard of!' roared one of the advisors indig-nantly."

The barber combed the coachman's bangs flat on his forehead. "A little shorter here in the front, right?"

Salim nodded. He didn't care. Now all he wanted was to know what happened to the impudent liar.

"So . . . as I was saying," Musa went on, "when the man said he had killed the angel of death, one of the more pious counselors cried out, 'Unheard of!' The other guests cried out, 'Liar!' The king thought and thought but he couldn't remember any number for this extraordinary lie: he had heard many lies about people outsmarting the angel of death, but no one had ever come upon the idea of killing him. While the king thought, the court fool stalled for time. 'You were there, too, weren't you,' he asked the man's wife and laughed.

"The woman didn't answer.

" 'Speak up, were you there or not!' commanded the king in an agitated voice.

" 'Your Grace! She cannot talk,' said the man. 'How could she? Since she saw me fighting with the angel of death she has been blind, deaf, and dumb.'

" 'You have won, I have never heard anything like that before. You shall receive your weight in gold,' spoke the king.

" 'Your Majesty, my time is still not up, and I have yet to release the biggest lie from its cage,' the man said with absolute tranquility. A whisper ran through the assembly.

" 'Very well,' said the king, 'but if the last grain of sand ends the hour and you have not succeeded in telling me a second new lie, then you shall lose your head.'

" 'I know what I'm doing. Have patience, O ruler

of the faithful. Well, after my battle with the angel of death, I was hungry. For three months we searched for food, in vain. Then we found a shriveled raisin. I used one third of it to quell my hunger. My wife ate the second third, and with the third third I opened a wine cellar not far from Aleppo. No matter how much I sold, the barrels stayed full.'

" 'Twenty-two!' the king called out.

" 'One day,' the man continued, 'I invited the king of Aleppo to my house. When he came I saw that he was troubled, and, crying, he explained to me that he was in love with a fish. But the fish did not requite his love, and in its pond it, too, was crying.'

" 'Six hundred fourteen,' the king triumphed and looked at the hourglass. Less than a quarter of an hour separated the man from his death.

" 'So the next day I went to the royal palace. There I knelt before the pond and called for the fish. It swam toward me, still crying. I asked why it was crying. "I want to go home," the fish answered. "The king is holding me prisoner here. I am not a fish, but a princess. What am I supposed to do with some stupid king who doesn't have anything better to do in his whole great kingdom than fall in love with fish? Set me free and you will not regret it. Kiss me!"

" 'Although I despise fish, I took it out of the water and kissed its slippery mouth—but instead of a princess I was holding a turtle. "Don't be disappointed,

young man," the turtle said, "I am a princess from the Isle of Wakwak. Whenever we travel abroad we change ourselves into turtles. Our homeland lives in us, and we live in it. Take me back to my homeland and my father will reward you richly!"

" 'We fled the palace under cover of darkness. I took leave of my wife, since she couldn't swim, and dove into the water. The turtle lay on my back and clamped its beak down tightly on my hair. It couldn't talk—this was a time when a single word was enough to cause death. I crossed the seven seas, and the turtle didn't say a word, but I heard its heart beating in the stillness of the oceans. On the seventh Sunday I sighted the Isle of Wakwak. There it was summer, while it was winter here.'

" 'One hundred forty-seven!' the king gloated.

" 'When we reached the calm water in the cove, the turtle said, "Thank you, good man!" I was frightened and spun around. A woman with the head and wings of a bird of paradise was slipping out of the turtle's shell. She rose into the air and flew before me. The Wakwakis are bird people. They have the heads and wings of birds but their bodies are human. I was received like a hero. They are very hospitable to strangers, above all if one arrives homeless and naked, as I did.

" 'At the same time, the land of the Wakwakis made me shudder: their sparrows were as big as our

elephants, and each one ate two lions for breakfast. Their crocodiles warbled like canaries, and their donkeys played the harp.'

" 'Four hundred three,' the king interjected curtly.

" 'And the way the Wakwakis ate, O king, I'm sure you've never heard about that. Lambs, chickens, geese, and pigs were running around and calling out, "Please, eat me! Please, enjoy me!" And when someone chose what he desired, after he had enjoyed the tender meat, he needed only to say to the bones, "Go! I've finished with you," and a fresh lamb, a goose, a chicken, or a pig would spring up and say, "Please, eat me!" '

" 'Six hundred twenty-two,' the king brushed the story aside.

" 'Well, the king of the Isle of Wakwak bestowed every possible honor upon me and showed me tremendous hospitality. As a reward for having saved the princess he gave me a telescope through which I could see the planets. I could even see the food on the tables of the alien beings.'

" 'Ninety-seven,' the king remarked.

" 'Now for the most important detail, my king. Guess who I met on the island?' the man asked, unperturbed.

" 'Me?' the king joked.

" 'No, your mother. She was there, in prison.'

" 'Your Majesty!' blurted one of the learned men.

176

'How much can your patience endure, the man is an unbelievable scoundrel!'

"But the queen mother, who was present, only smiled.

" 'Whether you believe it or not, O king, I freed her from prison with the thread of a spider and hid her in my palace, where my donkey drove away her sorrows with his harp.

" 'For fifteen days I was a guest on this island. My wife said I was away for fifteen years: well, of course a year of happiness passes more quickly than a day, and a night full of troubles becomes an eternity. During the fourteenth night I was sitting with your mother, O king. She was very sad. I asked her why. She sighed and looked at the donkey who was playing his harp for her. "Do you see this donkey?" she asked. "This donkey is smarter than my son!" '

" 'Shame upon you, you miserable boaster!' the queen mother now shouted in disgust.

"The king, however, held up his hand. 'Thirty-three,' was all he said.

" 'I didn't believe it either, but she replied, "You haven't met my son. If you are ever so unfortunate, you will understand my words. He really is dumber than a jackass." ' "

Musa took the large hairbrush and used it to brush the cuttings off the coachman's shoulders. He turned to Ali. "Pour some warm water from the kettle into

this bowl so that I can soap up this hedgehog.—So, the man called the king a jackass, and then he continued: 'Since I was extremely curious about my own country and its king, I decided to come back. I have to say that your mother was mistaken, for you, O king, have made your realm a paradise. At the gates of Damascus I saw two angels crying and looking very crestfallen. "Why are you crying?" I asked them.

" 'And they said to me: "Ever since King Sadek turned Damascus into such a glorious paradise, no one wants to come to us in Heaven anymore. We've lost our daily bread. O stranger, do not go in, have mercy on us and die before you enter Damascus."

" 'But I didn't have any desire to die just then, so I stepped through the East Gate into your glory. O king, right there at the gate, one of your soldiers stopped me, kissed me, and bid me welcome with bread and honey. I was amazed at this new custom, but the soldier said you had commanded it. People everywhere were glowing with happiness, and the poor were no longer receiving alms from your viziers, no, O king, for they had been given back their land, which you had divided among your followers long ago.'

" 'That's a lie,' the king cried out indignantly and immediately recognized his defeat.

" 'The man has won his weight in gold a second time,' chirped the fool, not without joy.

" 'The farmers received horses and tools so that

they could help themselves. Everything was so splendid, and every man so happy, that I just stood there, rooted to the earth in amazement. Then out of the blue a drunk ran right up to me and began to insult my mother and my father without the slightest reason. He was the son of this minister sitting on your right hand. But his noble background didn't help in the least, and a judge ordered him whipped. But before the sentence was carried out, the judge read him your law, O king, the one according to which even you should be whipped if you were to commit an injustice against any of your subjects.'

" 'That's a downright lie! I never passed any such law,' the king bellowed, and the guests roared. The jester stood on his head and cried out, 'Three times his weight in gold for this scoundrel. What a run of bad luck our king is having today!'

"The stranger went on with a straight face. 'O king, O creator of all good things in Damascus! I spent a whole day wandering about the city. When I asked passersby where I could find the prison, they simply laughed at me. What need for prisons in paradise? Children heard the word *hunger* for the first time from my lips. May my tongue be torn from my mouth for having bruised their delicate ears. Yes, without a doubt, I told my wife, I would like to be the king of such a country. Everything works as if guided by the hands of angels. If I were king in such a land, I would be free from all worry and would pass

the time listening to lies and letting gold flow and heads roll. Why not?

" 'But your mother's words would not let me rest. I had to see for myself why your mother had cursed you, for it is rare indeed that a mother will speak badly of her own children to strangers. So I went to the palace guard and demanded an audience. The king will not receive a mangy dog like you, replied the watchman. Nonetheless, I strode right through the gate with my head held high. The watchman raised his sword and let it fall upon me. How on earth did the poor fellow know that this was the one day I had forgotten to rub myself with the ant's milk. The sword landed on my head and I keeled over dead.'

" 'You're lying,' cried the king. 'You're still alive!'

" 'Four times in gold,' shouted the fool.

" 'Alive?' said the man. 'You call this being alive? Forgive me, O king, your mother was right after all!'

"The stranger stood up and, together with his wife, walked away.

" 'But wait! You have won four times your weight in gold!' cried the king. But the man did not turn back, not even once.

"So that's my story. Now I have entrusted it to you, keep it safe and tell it to the next person. And as for you, my dear Salim, I have shaved your beard without a single cut. Isn't that amazing?"

When Salim got up, Ali took the newspaper,

which was covered with cut hair, rolled it into a ball, and carried it out to the trash.

"Are you tired?" asked Tuma. But Salim felt refreshed after his shave. The friends sat together for a long time and amused themselves by comparing examples of the government's lies.

When the clock tower struck twelve, Musa yawned aloud. Isam placed three cards on the table. "There aren't many left!" he noted.

Ali leaned back. "You are the oldest of the three of us. If there really is such a thing as respect for age, the ace should jump into your hand." The former minister smiled and nodded, for he, too, was happy to let Isam go first. Isam studied the three cards and chose the one on the right.

It was indeed the ace of spades. Far off in the distance they heard thunder, as if wild horsemen were galloping toward Damascus.

10

*How
one man bit
his own eye and caused
another man to change his view*

Isam, the former prisoner, really didn't need to busy himself with vegetables, chickpeas, and cheap songbirds. By the time he was released, his two sons had grown up and become respected auto mechanics. Their shop was known throughout Damascus. The two brothers also owned a large house with a garden in the fashionable Salihiya district, and Isam and his wife lived in one wing of this mansion. Their sons saw to their parents' every need. A housekeeper cared for them as devotedly as if she were their own daughter. The brothers begged Isam to rest after the hardships he had endured in prison, and to enjoy himself. But he cast all their entreaties to the wind and refused to give up his trading. Out of love for his sons, and so that no one would speak ill of them, Isam confined his peddling to the more remote streets of Damascus. However, rain was the only thing that could keep him from going to the Friday market to sell his songbirds.

While Isam's generous hand earned him a good

name as a vegetable dealer, his reputation on the bird market was not exactly pristine. People in the know branded him a "dyer," because Isam dyed cheap songbirds to enhance their appearance. Some birds were given a bath in yellow or orange dye, so that they wound up looking like poor cousins of canaries. Others received an exotic mix of several dyes, and then only the most fantastic names could do justice to their colorful plumage—Prince of Brazil, King Redhead, and Rainbowbird were some of Isam's favorites.

Isam made the most money selling goldfinches, which are highly prized in Damascus—that is, when they're mature. Young specimens aren't worth a thing; all they do is eat and produce piles of droppings, and maybe emit a pitiful peep or two if they happen to be hungry. Not until they're at least a year old, when they show a red circle around their beak, are they considered full-grown, and then they are expensive, for then they sing delightfully. Isam sped up this natural process by furnishing young birds with a premature red circle around the beak; he would then sell them at bargain prices to novice collectors. Of course, these unsuspecting souls were convinced that they had gotten the better of some poor old fool, and they would race home with their newly acquired goldfinch. But then they waited and waited for the bird to sing and wondered why the circle around the beak was growing paler and paler—and why the drinking water in the little bowl was growing redder and redder.

On this day Isam arrived carrying an impressive cage. When he entered the room he set off a storm of laughter.

"No, no—this one's real!" he shouted. "A magnificent goldfinch. My son had his eye on this one, but I am bringing it to Salim. May he speak as beautifully as this wonderful bird can sing. And may God protect him from the envious!"

The friends were so moved they didn't know whether to laugh or cry. The small songbird didn't keep them waiting long: as soon as Isam had hung the cage from a hook on the wall, it started warbling away.

Salim smiled with delight and handed his friend a glass of tea.

Isam sat down on the sofa and was silent for a while. Salim was already rubbing his hands in anticipation, and instead of taking the free chair next to the sofa, he crouched on the floor at the feet of his guests. He looked at Isam expectantly.

"You know," Isam said to him, "I spent twelve years in solitary confinement. The cell was dark even in the middle of the day. Who are you supposed to tell stories to there? If you had paper, you could at least tell them to the paper, but what are you going to tell to four damp and dirty walls? Besides, at the

time I could neither read nor write. And last night I was barely able to sleep. You know, I was thinking about how long I've been alive. I'm sixty-eight years old, but really I'm just fifty-six, since those twelve years can't count as life at all."

Isam began to choke with emotion, and Salim placed his hand on his friend's knee.

"Salim, you are wonderful! You know, your hands can speak, even if your tongue cannot. There was this man I knew in prison. He was mute, but we understood his words through his hands.—But now on to me! When I was a child I loved to sing. Everyone liked my voice, and I was always allowed to sing in the mosque and at weddings, and whenever I sang, people cried and said that someday I would be a famous singer. But one day, all that came to an end. Who was going to believe me—when there I was, standing right beside my cousin's body, and holding the knife?

"I had never forgiven him for humiliating me in front of the whole bazaar. But my wife said it was wrong for cousins to carry on a feud like that, and since I was the younger, it was my place to try to patch things up. You know, my cousin was convinced that I had swindled him out of all that money. And I could see why he thought that way, too. I mean, I was a pretty sly devil in those days."

"You still are!" joked Musa.

"Maybe so, but only at the Friday market—back

then I was one every day. But I didn't swindle him at all."

"How so?" asked Junis.

"We—a man from Aleppo named Ismail, my cousin, and myself—had found a treasure. The man had read in one of his secret books that a large urn filled with gold coins was buried in my cousin's courtyard. Supposedly it had been hidden there by some Ottoman officer who was fleeing the French. The officer figured he would, you know, sneak back once everything had settled down. But then a cholera epidemic came and snatched him away along with his entire family. Ismail claimed to have been his servant, but today I'm sure that he was the devil in person. How else could he have picked me out from among the thousands of people in Damascus? You know, to this day I get goose bumps whenever I mention his name. Here, just look. The devil himself, I tell you. You know, we first met next to the Takiya Suleimaniya, right where the man who had built the mosque jumped to his death. Of course, that should have told me that nothing good could come of it, but I was still young and stupid."

"What are you talking about?" asked the emigrant, somewhat confused.

"You don't know the story of the mosque?" When the emigrant shook his head, Isam went on: "The great Ottoman sultan Suleiman commissioned a famous master, by the name of Sinan, to build a mosque

and a dormitory for dervishes on pilgrimage. Sinan worked day and night for years and years until he finally completed the beautiful mosque. The sultan visited the mosque with his courtiers and was pleased. He praised the master's work, and especially the slender minaret. Sinan then recounted for his patron the trials and tribulations he had had to endure to erect that minaret. The guests clapped their hands and hailed the sultan and his great master builder. But then, all of a sudden, this old man spoke up and said in a very matter-of-fact voice, 'Trials and tribulations my foot! A minaret like that is child's play!' The sultan had the old man brought before him—he turned out to be a journeyman who had worked for Sinan the builder.

" 'Child's play?' repeated the sultan. 'Woe unto you, you shameless old fool! I shall give you one year to build a similar minaret, and if you don't succeed, then off with your head!'

" 'One month is all I need!' answered the old journeyman. 'Take master Sinan with you, so he doesn't see anything, and in one month have him brought here blindfolded. If he can tell which minaret is his, then I shall gladly pay with my life.'

" 'Master Sinan will be my guest for one month. But woe betide you, old man, if you have let your envy lead you astray,' said the sultan, who then journeyed with the master builder to his palace in the north.

"After exactly one month, the sultan, his guests, and the builder Sinan traveled back to Damascus. Crowds thronged the main square, itching with curiosity. You know, the people were standing so close together that if you had dropped a tiny needle from the minaret, it wouldn't have reached the ground, it would have got stuck on one of the thousands and thousands of heads.

"Sultan Suleiman was famous for his fairness. He held to the conditions of the bet and kept the master builder blindfolded until they were all standing on a platform in front of the mosque. Then the master turned pale, because the two minarets were mirror images. He rubbed his eyes, but he couldn't tell which of the two spires was his.

" 'I have to climb up; it's easier for me to tell from up there,' Sinan said and hurried up one of the minarets. He was sure he would find some of his secret marks. You know, some of the stones had notches, and he had painted a few of the tiles himself. When he reached the top, he saw the stones and the tiles and was about to announce that this minaret was his, when he suddenly glanced over and saw the same stones and tiles on the minaret's twin. He hurried down and climbed up the second tower. There, too, he found his signature. Sinan stood on top of the tower, looking down at the crowd, which began to jeer at him. He cried out so loud that the earth shook,

then cursed the old journeyman and leaped to his death."

"That's not true," the minister interrupted. "After the mosque in Damascus, the great master Sinan went on to build many wonderful mosques, both large and small, including the one at Edirne in Turkey. My father once took me there. A dream in paint and stone, shadow and light. The man found murdered here under the minarets the day after their unveiling was a dervish in love with the daughter of the regent of Damascus. He used to visit her secretly at night in the garden of the mosque. It's a sad story. I was . . ."

"What does it matter?" Isam picked up where he had left off. "In any case, it was on that spot where I met this devil. He knew more about me than my parents. He told me our stars had met in heaven. You know, words know how to tickle better than fingers. And his words were so clever and so sweet, he could have moved a hippopotamus to sprout wings and fly! He claimed that my cousin had been born under an unlucky star, and so he should stay out of the house on the day we dug up the treasure, otherwise his presence might turn the gold coins into snakes—but he would still receive his third of the treasure.

"Now, my cousin was always suspicious of everybody. He was afraid that Ismail was out to swindle us, but I convinced him otherwise, and so he took his wife and child and left the house. Then this devil and I started digging; from dawn until noon we shoveled out a tremendous hole in the middle of the courtyard where the treasure was supposed to be, but we didn't find anything. At noon we ate some bread with cheese and olives—I remember to this day—and after that I made some tea. Then I had to use the bathroom.

"When I came back, there was this devil, calm as could be, sitting there sipping his tea and talking about his travels. I sat down under an orange tree and drank the tea without the slightest suspicion. It tasted good. All of a sudden I felt this strange drowsiness start to overpower me. I staggered into the kitchen and doused my head with cold water, but I couldn't make it back outside. Then everything went dark, but I could still hear this devil laughing loudly.

"When I came to, the man was long gone. The shards of a great clay urn were lying scattered on the pile of dirt. On a flat stone I found two gold Ottoman liras. Without thinking, I put them in my pocket.

"When my cousin came back I was still groggy. 'So where's my share?' he asked, when he saw the shards.

"I was a complete wreck. 'Ismail drugged me and took off with the money,' I answered. My cousin grabbed hold of me and tore off my pants and shirt. The two gold liras came tumbling out of my pocket. Now there was no man on earth who could prove to him that I had fallen into the scoundrel's trap just like

he had. As far as he was concerned, those two gold liras were more than enough evidence of my guilt. He pounded away at me without mercy, and if the neighbors hadn't come to my aid I would have been a dead man. But he didn't stop there! He slandered me everywhere he went, so that people avoided me like the plague.

"One Friday I went to the mosque. When I came out he beat me once again, right in front of all the believers, and this time no one bothered to help me. I cursed him and swore I would kill him. For three months we didn't say a word to each other. But then the Feast of Sacrifice was coming up, and my wife said it wasn't right that we should begin the holy days full of hate. So I made my way to his house.

"When I pushed open the door, none of his family came to greet me. I called out for him, but everything was quiet. I called out again. Then I heard someone gasping in the kitchen. I ran there right away, and found my cousin lying on his stomach in a pool of blood. I turned him over, but it was too late. He died in my arms, without saying a word. The knife was lying next to him. I started to run out to the courtyard and call the neighbors for help, but all of a sudden his wife and younger son appeared in the kitchen doorway. The woman stood there, frozen. She looked at my hands and clothes smeared with blood and started screaming. To this day I don't know why, but I picked up the knife and started to stammer: 'With

. . . the knife . . .' That was it. For the judges it was clear as day that I had done the deed."

"And why did the real murderer do it?" asked Faris.

"The devil only knows! My cousin was always getting into tangles with people. He wasn't a very pleasant man. I later found out that he had hired this murderer to beat up a certain highly respected merchant. This thug had come to collect, and my cousin tried to throw him out. He was always setting people like that on his opponents, but he never let them come to his house, to keep everything secret."

"Then what happened?" Ali wanted to know.

"No, let's get on with your story," the teacher interjected.

"Story?—Oh, that's right, I wanted to tell you about one of my fellow prisoners who never wanted to bet."

"Just a minute!" Ali interrupted.

Musa sided with the locksmith. "The night is long," he said, "we'll get to that story, but first I want to know what happened to you next. We've known one another for years, and you've never told us any of this before. In this blessed night you have opened your heart. Finish telling us about yourself. That's more important than some story or other."

Isam looked at Salim. "Aren't you tired of all this dumb stuff I'm telling about myself?"

Salim smiled, pressed his friend's hand and gave a sign as if to say, "Go ahead, there's no rush."

"So, then hell opened its gates for me. For twelve years the prison warden—may God rain curses upon him—kept me locked up in a basement, until I looked exactly like the monster he imagined I was. Not until after his death—and may his soul languish and broil in hell—did the new warden have me taken to a group cell. That's where I spent the second half of my time. It was a lot easier than the hell of solitary confinement. You know, when you don't talk for years, even your dreams become mute. Your words wilt and rot inside your mouth. The only company I had in that hole were the rats. Sometimes I wished they would attack me and put an end to my misery, but they showed me more mercy than the human beings did. You can't imagine how it tormented me that I was the only one who knew I was innocent. It's true, my wife *believed* I was, and she stood loyally by my side, but I was the only one who really knew."

"And your friends?" asked Faris.

Isam smiled bitterly. "Oh, my friends believed me, all right, at least at first, but later they believed the judges. And after I was sent away, did they even once look in on my wife? No, they just left her in the lurch, with two sons to raise, all by herself. Meanwhile, I was sitting in prison and the thought that she was suffering along with me was more than I could bear. You know, there were times when I even hated the fact she was so loyal.

"And then there were times when I felt this fire in my head—you know, a fire that wants to burst out. It kept burning inside me, and even when I was so exhausted I just keeled over, it continued to smolder. I would suddenly wake up and start to hurl myself against the walls and howl like some wild animal, until the fire went out.

"When I was finally moved to a cell with other people I felt reborn. The fire never burned my soul again. Of course, life there was difficult enough: we were often beaten, you know, back then. Whenever they brought someone back half dead, we gave him cigarettes and tea and sang to him, and then his wounded face would slowly break out in a smile. That's when we knew that we had beaten the guards.

"There was this poet who served five years with us because of a song, and he taught me how to read and write. We became good friends. He had read thousands of books in his life, and I was as thirsty as a sponge. I was able to teach him a few things as well. He spent too much time brooding; the only reason he managed to cope was because the others felt sorry for him. I taught him how to wangle cigarettes, tea, and even arak. He was a good pupil. First he watched me do it, and then he went at it. He wound up winning the respect of the worst thugs; besides, they needed his advice. He knew more than a lawyer, you know,

and in prison only one out of a hundred inmates could read. Even years after his release he used to visit me every week, until he was forced to leave the country.

"But that's enough babble about me! Now I want to tell you a real story. As God is my witness, I will tell you only what Ahmad told me.

"The prisoners all liked to gamble. You know, it's a good way to kill time, and you can also win a little tea, a few cigarettes, or a piece of bread. But we had this one prisoner who never bet. His name was Ahmad. We would be gambling away like mad, and he would just sit in the corner like a stone. He was dirt poor, and whenever I won something I gave part of it to him. Now, I'm not one to pry, but one day I asked him why he never played along. 'Why don't you ever bet?' I said. Well, you know in the beginning I thought he was a miser, but actually he was very generous. There was this one time I had a run of bad cards and lost everything I had after just a few hands. Bankrupt. So I was sitting down in the corner next to him, and he took off his new shirt and gave it to me, without saying a word. I traded the shirt for three boxes of cigarettes, and then I was able to win back everything I had lost. But he himself never gambled.

"We would bet on anything. Sometimes, if we couldn't find anything better, someone would holler: 'Any bets on whether this fly's going to land on my nose?' and we'd all rush to place our bets. There were tricks, you know, that you could use to influence the fly. If you brush a fly off in a certain way—just a little bit, not too much—it will come back to the same spot as if it owned it."

"I know about those damned rascals! Whenever one takes a fancy to my nose, it always ruins my nap," Musa confirmed with a laugh.

"I can tell you," Isam continued, "that you go into prison with one profession and come out with a thousand and one professions. You can learn anything there. I told you how I learned to read. You can become a baker, a butcher, or a locksmith like Ali here, but that's not all—you also learn how to use a knife, how to counterfeit money, how to smuggle, and how to tell jokes. You want to hear a joke?"

"Let's hear it," said Tuma encouragingly.

"This is a political joke I heard from that poet I was talking about. The only jokes he told were political. Well, this joke goes like this: there are these two assassins hiding right outside the presidential palace. They're waiting for the president to come out, and their fingers are glued to the triggers of their pistols. Well the whole day goes by, but this president never leaves the palace. So the assassins keep waiting. The next day comes and goes, and still no sign of the president. Then the third day comes and the same thing happens. By now the men are pretty upset.

" 'Where the hell can he be?' asks one.

"The other man turns to his companion, full of concern, and says, 'God, I hope nothing's happened to him!'

"We used to tell jokes all the time. The guards treated us worse than animals, you know, but we just laughed at them—among ourselves, that is. You want to hear another joke about the guards?"

"No, no, why don't you tell us about this man who didn't want to bet," the minister requested impatiently. He was the only one who hadn't laughed at the joke.

"Right. Let's see. His name was Ahmad. Once I asked him why he never bet. Right, I said that. Oh. So once he told me his story. It was incredible, like many of the prisoners' stories. You know, you hear a lot of stories in prison. Fifty percent you throw overboard, and another thirty percent you're bound to forget. But what's left is still unbelievable. Absolutely unbelievable! There was this Armenian serving a year's sentence. His name was Mehran. A small guy —short, and skinny as a rail. When we asked him what he had been sent up for, all he said was: 'Beat up big bear.' He didn't speak Arabic very well. It took us a month to put together what had happened. Apparently he had this neighbor who was as big and strong as our Ali, and the man used to beat his children every afternoon. Mehran asked him to stop because he— Mehran, that is—wanted to enjoy his afternoon nap, and besides, he couldn't stand children being beaten.

So this big bear of a neighbor growls back that from then on not only would he beat his children, but Mehran as well. Then he went after Mehran, but Mehran caught him with his right hand and hurled him several yards. And the bear wound up in the hospital.

"Judges don't understand beans. The neighbor should have gone to prison, not this Armenian. But what am I going on about? You know, they stole so many years of my life . . . but we don't want to be sad. Now where was I?"

"About the brave Armenian?" said Ali the locksmith.

"About Ahmad! You were going to tell us why he never bet," the minister grumbled.

Isam looked at Faris a little confused. "That's right, about Ahmad, but let me say just one more thing about the Armenian. Like I was saying, Mehran was not very big. When we finally understood what he was saying, we all laughed and figured he was just a pickpocket. Pickpockets aren't exactly respected in prison, you know, so they always try to make up stories to impress the others. But one day we were in the yard when these two thugs decided to pick on him, just like that, for no good reason—I mean, Mehran, he wouldn't even harm a fly. He never started a fight in all his life. But if someone did him wrong, Mehran never forgave him. He could carry a grudge longer than a camel. In any case, there were

these two big thugs out in the yard who could eat him for breakfast, so to speak, without a swallow of tea, and they attacked him. Mehran stood his ground, firm as a rock, and then quick as lightning he flipped the first man, just like a pea, right into the second. Those two thugs went limping around for weeks.

"The strange thing was, though, that Mehran didn't want to be the boss of the cell. The strongest man we had was this boy from Homs. When he saw what Mehran had done he told him right then and there he would give up his place by the window. But, you know, Mehran declined. He didn't want to be anybody's boss."

"His mother must have fed him lion's milk for breakfast," commented the barber.

"Armenians are very brave," Junis confirmed. "I knew one named Karabet. He came to my coffee-house every day. His Arabic was no better than this Mehran's, but each word was like a whole story. One day—" Junis wanted to go on, but by then the minister had lost his patience entirely.

"And Ahmad, what finally happened with your goddamned Ahmad?" he groaned.

"You're right," said Isam. "I really have to get to Ahmad. When Ahmad was young, he was famous for having a keen nose for wagers and a nimble tongue. He made a lot of money off his poor neighbors whom he drew into his bets. He was such a good talker that the president invited him to his parties in order to

keep the guests entertained. There wasn't a better joke teller in the whole prison. But that wasn't all his tongue was good for; it was every bit as sharp as a dagger of Damascus steel. Only Abu Nuwas in his day could be as sharp as that—do you know his story about the chickens and the caliph?"

"No, what story is that?" Tuma wanted to know, but now the minister was rolling his eyes.

"Please, I beg you," said Faris emphatically, "for a few piasters you can buy Abu Nuwas's story of the chickens and the caliph in the bookstore. Let's get back to this damned Ahmad, or whoever he was."

"Of course, you're right, I'm sorry. I will now swear by the soul of my mother that I will finish the story of Ahmad. Where was I. Oh. Right. One day the president and his wife hosted a benefit for poor orphans. For weeks the newspapers wrote about the upcoming event; anybody who was anybody was supposed to be there—the richest merchants, the wealthiest farmers, the heads of the most powerful families, writers, actors, and foreign guests were all going to take part.

"The food was out of this world. The tables were piled high with roast gazelle, peacock liver pâté, and pistachio rolls, and the guests applauded the dancers, singers, and jugglers. Well, the president started drinking a lot and, you know, whenever the president was drunk it was dangerous to go near him,

there was no telling what he might do. I heard once that he had been invited to Malula and—"

"Blessed be the soul of your mother!" reminded Faris.

"Oh, right, that's another story. Well, the president was drinking away when he suddenly remembered Ahmad. He sent for him and spoke to him angrily: 'These guests are all miserly locusts. They're picking the tables clean and the only thing they're offering is their applause! It's a disgrace! And in front of foreign ambassadors! Use your tongue, bigmouth, and see to it that you pull every last piaster out of their pockets, otherwise I'm going to banish you to the desert.'

"Ahmad just smiled. He climbed onstage and addressed the audience: 'Esteemed ladies and gentlemen. Because the contributions are below expectations, our Most Beloved has decided to donate what every man holds most dear: a hair from his moustache.'

"The president stood up and applauded this stroke of genius. A woman in a white dress carrying a small red pillow approached His Excellency. He bent down, and she plucked a hair from his moustache. When the guests saw the president twitch, they all clapped, without realizing they had fallen into a trap.

" 'And now His Excellency would like to know exactly how much the esteemed guests love him. He is putting up for auction one hair of his moustache, and he is anxious to discover how much the noble hair will bring. Whoever wishes to participate in the bidding must pay one gold lira—just raise your hand. And now, let the bidding begin! With a little luck, the most noble hair in the world will belong to you!'

"The guests grew silent. They looked at one another at a loss as to what to do, but then someone raised his hand and offered a hundred gold liras. No luck—his neighbor was already offering a hundred fifty. The first man paid his gold lira and leaned back in his chair, but the bidding didn't stop at a hundred fifty. Next thing you know, people were calling out one thousand, three thousand, six thousand. A team of girls and boys collected the gold liras from those present, and the auction continued. Soon you could hear bids of twenty thousand, even a hundred thousand. The shouting grew louder and louder and angrier and angrier, since everyone now wanted to prove that he loved the president most. Not until three hours later did Ahmad call out: 'Three hundred thousand going once, going twice—sold for three hundred thousand liras! Sir, my congratulations! The noble hair belongs to you. What a prize!' Everyone strained his neck to see who Ahmad was congratulating. It was an ironmonger from Damascus. He went up and accepted the small pillow a little uncertainly. All the guests applauded, although a few felt sincerely sorry for the man.

"No sooner had everyone recovered from all that

than Ahmad again walked onto the stage and shouted into the hall: 'His Excellency is pleased with his guests, so he has decided to liven up the evening with a few bets. His Excellency enjoys a little wager now and then. His Excellency would like to bet that no one present will box him on the ear. Whoever dares try will receive one hundred gold liras. Everyone else will again lose one gold lira!' Of course, most of the guests there would have gladly boxed the president three hundred times for that low-down idea, but no one dared try. So they paid one lira apiece, but in their hearts they cursed the soul of the president's father for the way he had reared his son.

" 'Shall we now bet,' Ahmad called out to his president's applause, 'that I can devise a riddle that none of you can solve? His Excellency will permit me to offer half a million gold liras from the National Bank to anyone who can solve the riddle.'

" 'Half a million?'—'What kind of riddle?'—'Does the National Bank even have that much money?'

"The guests saw the president laugh and nod his head.

" 'Esteemed ladies and gentlemen: I will satisfy your curiosity, but bear in mind, if no one can solve the riddle, then everyone must donate ten gold liras to the Orphans' Fund.'

" 'Go ahead and give us the damned riddle,' someone called out from one of the back rows. The guests laughed and admired the man's courage.

" 'What person,' Ahmad asked, 'can bite his own eye?' Now it was the president's turn to laugh, which he did, slapping his thigh with gusto.

" 'Don't feel bad!' Ahmad consoled the angry public. 'Although none of you can win this bet, you will definitely win the love of the orphans.'

" 'That's not true. I can do it!' a voice cried out. The hall fell deadly silent. The same ironmonger as before stood up.

" 'My good man, no one on earth can do that!' Ahmad laughed out loud.

" 'I can. I can bite both my right eye and my left!' the man shouted back.

" 'Well, then, please come up here and show us how you can bite your own eyes,' Ahmad said to the man with pity in his voice.

"The man climbed onstage and turned to face the guests. 'Here is my right eye!' he said, and he pulled the eye out of its socket and held it up with two fingers. The whole audience gasped, and one or two ladies fainted. Then the man guided the eye into his mouth.

" 'But that's not your real eye—it's made of glass,' Ahmad said with a note of triumph. Most of the guests were still confused, but a couple of people laughed.

"The ironmonger remained undaunted. 'Very well,' he said, 'I can also bite my left eye, and that one is real.' He opened his mouth and took out his false

teeth. He snapped them in the air once or twice and then used them to bite his left eye. The guests all whooped with joy—and Ahmad turned pale as a sheet. Because of the foreign ambassadors present, the president had no choice but to pay. And for that he had Ahmad jailed for life.

"I'm sure you remember the time when that president miraculously survived his first assassination attempt and he declared a general amnesty. Well, he even let child murderers out of prison, but not Ahmad.

"He was a good man, this Ahmad, and he was as sharp as they come. Once the chief warden showed up late in the night and ordered us to clean the cell. He kept yelling at us to make the floor shine or else he'd make us lick it spic and span. I asked him for the reason.

" 'The president,' said the warden, 'is coming here tomorrow at ten o'clock in the morning.'

"Ahmad looked at the warden in amazement. 'What's that?' he asked. 'You mean you finally caught the scoundrel?'

"Well, that's it, that's my story. I hope you found it somewhat entertaining."

"My dear," the minister yawned, "that was a thousand and one stories." Then he grinned.

"But be happy," Musa teased Isam, "because if you really were Scheherazade, you would have used up every last one of your stories the first night."

Salim just smiled, stood up, walked over to Isam, and kissed his friend on his moustache.

Isam laughed. He took the two remaining cards and laid them down before the locksmith and the minister. "I'm anxious to know which of you two gentlemen will be our Scheherazade tomorrow night." He gestured for them each to choose a card.

"Well, Excellency, it looks like your turn tomorrow," Ali said happily when the minister drew the ace.

11

*How
one man
had to hear after death
what he had been deaf to while alive*

Faris, the former minister, came from an old landed Damascus family. His father had received the honorary title Pasha from the sultan in Istanbul as a reward for his loyalty to the Ottoman Empire—which invented strange titles by the dozen. But this pasha was a sly old fox. He sensed that the days of the Ottoman Empire were numbered, and so he began to put out feelers toward France. The French consul was a more and more frequent guest, and eventually the pasha became the first confidant of the French representatives who soon replaced the Ottoman regime in Syria. But the seasoned pasha knew that the French, too, would not stay in Syria forever. While continuing to receive the French governor, he secretly funded several nationalist groups, whose clamors for independence were growing louder and louder.

This was how the pasha thought and acted until the day he died, and there were many stories about his shrewdness.

Throughout his long life he was a faithful Muslim, and as such he made the pilgrimage to Mecca many times. There, at Mount Arafat, all pilgrims are supposed to pelt the devil with seven small symbolic stones. The pasha was very meticulous in observing all the other rites, but when it came to the stoning of the Evil One he cast only six pebbles.

"And why don't you throw the seventh stone?" his friends asked him every time.

"I don't want to spoil my relationship with the devil completely," he is said to have answered.

Two days before independence the old man died, but his title lived on in the family for decades, even though the Ottoman Empire had long since collapsed.

Faris was the pasha's youngest, and most sensitive, son. Because he seemed totally unsuited to business as well as farming, his father sent him to study law at the Sorbonne in Paris, so that he could later represent the interests of the family.

The late pasha's wish seemed fulfilled when Faris became a member of the first independent government of Syria. However, instead of administering his office with the benign neglect expected of him, Faris proceeded to nationalize the electric works, the tobacco industry, and other important enterprises. His family was enraged. The working classes hailed the new minister as the "Red Pasha," although all they really gained were higher prices for tobacco, water, electricity, and other products of the newly nationalized industries, which they now ostensibly owned.

Nevertheless, people appreciated Faris' populist gestures. While in office, Faris declined to have bodyguards and chauffeurs like the other ministers. Every morning, he left his house at eight o'clock and walked through the bazaar to his ministry, which he reached at a little after nine. "In the bazaar," he explained, "I can smell how the people are doing."

At the end of March 1949, a certain colonel, equipped with a few antiquated tanks and jeeps, took over the presidential residence. At dawn his followers tore the president from his bed and deposed him. They then moved quickly on to the radio station, where they had to rouse the sleeping doorman. "This is a coup d'état for freedom and against Zionism," their leader screamed at the doorman, "Syria is on the brink of ruin, and the politicians are to blame!" The poor doorman had no idea what a coup d'état was, because this was the first, not only in Syria but in all Arabia, and with great concern he turned to the leader and asked: "But what's going to happen to my pension?"

A few minutes after six o'clock the colonel informed the populace, and the whole world, of his honorable intentions; half an hour later he drove to see Faris, whom he knew quite well. The Red Pasha was still asleep, but the impertinent colonel saw to it that he was awakened. Still wearing his pyjamas, Faris entered his large salon, where the colonel was sitting on the sofa with outspread legs. Two younger officers were standing on either side.

"Well, how do you like my coup? Not a single drop of blood spilled. Isn't it a stroke of genius?"

"Excellency, is that your reason for waking me up?" Faris asked sleepily.

"Yes, absolutely—I want to hear what you think."

"If you want to hear what I think, then first send these officers outside. I will not have armed hoodlums breaking into my house," Faris answered sullenly.

The officers protested, but their commander calmed them down and they went out.

"Now, tell me, isn't it magnificent?"

"Of course, Excellency, of course. Except you have opened a door in Syria that you will never again be able to close. What's more, you have dragged me from my bed. And now you had better beware, because the day will come sooner than you think when you will be dragged from yours."

"I'm no civilian," the officer laughed. "I sleep in my uniform, and my pistol never sleeps at all," he said and went outside.

No one in Damascus knows whether or not this conversation actually took place. But two things are certain: Faris was removed from office, and one unbearably hot August night the colonel was arrested by new conspirators, who also wanted nothing less than to save Syria from ruin. The colonel, the brilliant author of the first putsch, ruled for only one hundred thirty-four days. He was dragged from his bed and shot in a suburb of Damascus—in his pyjamas, no less.

And the door he had opened in Syria was not shut for many years.

Faris decided never again to join a government. He earned a fortune practicing law and became a respected legal authority. Many judges were supposedly convinced that he would soon be reappointed minister. He never ruled out the possibility, and that only increased his stature in the judges' eyes, so that they were inclined to pay closer attention to his presentations than to those of his opponents.

On this evening, he was the first to arrive, but he looked sleepy. "Do you have any strong coffee?" he asked Salim, who hurried into the kitchen and fixed him a strong mocha. Then the other gentlemen came in, one by one.

"Your stories," said Faris, "have robbed me of my sleep. Last night I was sitting on my terrace, wondering: Why do people tell stories? What *is* storytelling, anyway? I racked my brains until early in the morning.

"I recalled that when I was minister I knew this old man. He used to bring me my coffee every morning, and every day he told me a little story, just for fun. Unfortunately I never really listened. All I managed to retain were a few bits and pieces, but now when I think of them I find them full of wisdom. It's a pity I didn't know how to listen back in those days. You know, I think all rulers are incapable of listening while they're in power.

"I didn't tell stories, either, in those days. I just had my colleagues, clients, and lackeys tell me what they wanted, as concisely as possible, and then I made my decisions. If I spoke at all, it was only to issue an order. This morning I asked my wife over breakfast when it was that I started telling stories, and she said, 'Ever since you were so rudely ousted from your office, you've been downright talkative.' To me, it's no surprise that rulers who have lost their power suddenly begin to talk and write volumes about their lives.

"Tonight, if you will lend me your patience and your ears, I want to tell you a story about one ruler who never listened, a story that is both extremely funny and very wise."

Just when the minister was about to begin, the goldfinch woke up and started singing loudly. Isam could not restrain a triumphant laugh.

"Once upon a time," Faris began, but the goldfinch twittered more, and even more loudly.

"Cover the cage so the canary will sleep," Musa groaned.

"It's a goldfinch. And look, it wants to tell a story, too," Isam defended his protégé, and as if the bird had understood his words, it began blithely warbling away.

"If you don't cover that damned bird, I won't be able to tell you anything," said Faris. Salim, who

could taste the seriousness of his words, quickly threw a black kerchief over the cage.

"Once upon a time, or perhaps in never-never-land," Faris began again, "in any case, in days of yore, there lived a king. His kingdom lay farther than the Isle of Wakwak. His face was so round and so bright, it could have said to the full moon on a summer evening: 'Climb down, so I can take your place and charm the people on earth.' Though he was very young when he succeeded his father, the new king was smarter than a snake and slier than a fox, and he assembled only the most cunning ministers, who ruled the kingdom with an iron hand. The year he ascended to the throne he married a princess, whose grace turned the very roses of Damascus pale with envy."

"That was beautifully said," whispered Mehdi the teacher.

Musa the barber voiced his reaction as well: "A few weeks with a girl like that would make me younger by a few years."

"And what would you do with your false teeth?" jabbed Isam.

"In any case," the minister went on, "the king wanted a son. But his wife gave birth to a daughter. And even though she surpassed her mother in beauty, the king looked on his child and broke into a rage. With tears in his eyes, he gave the order to have them

both taken to a distant island. Throughout his kingdom, however, he had it proclaimed that the queen had died in childbirth."

"God should have crippled the tongue of this heartless man for such a lie!" shouted Junis the café owner.

"Cowardly dog," Musa vented his own anger. "What does he have against a daughter? I have five of them, and I wouldn't trade their tiniest toenail for a son."

"Just a minute, now. I have six sons, and each one is a lion—" the locksmith objected.

"And that's exactly what the king wanted," said the minister, returning to his story, "but his second wife also bore him a daughter. She, too, was removed, to an even more distant island. The third," the minister laughed, "the fourth, the fifth, the sixth . . ." He was laughing so hard he choked and had to clear his throat.

"This king's beginning to get a little boring," said Tuma, as if he wanted to ask the minister what he was finding so funny.

"All right, now it gets really funny," said the minister. "With every passing year, the king grew angrier and angrier. He listened less and less to his ministers and least of all to his jester. In the seventh year of his reign, he married a woman known for her shrewdness. She, too, became pregnant, but in her eighth month—it was already summer—she told her hus-

band she wanted to move to the summer palace, since it was too hot in the capital for her to rest. No sooner said than done, and off she drove into the refreshing climate of the mountains, accompanied only by her loyal handmaid.

"As soon as the queen began her labor, messengers from the king arrived, ready to race back to the palace with good news or bad. For three days and three nights they waited outside the queen's chamber, to become either the doves of good tidings or the hyenas of bad."

"Well said, may God bless your mouth!" said Mehdi.

"And yours," the minister replied and continued: "Late in the afternoon on the third day the messengers heard the newborn cry and the handmaid give a joyful shout. After a short while she came outside, her eyes flooded with tears. 'Tell our most beloved lord to cast off all his worries'—she was sobbing with joy —'for Heaven has granted his wish and given us all a strong and sturdy prince!'

"The king was ecstatic to hear that his heart's desire had been fulfilled, and he received the queen with great pomp and circumstance. Thousands of his subjects thronged to greet her. From his balcony the ruler held up his successor—whom he named Ahmad —for all to see. The whole land went giddy with joy. A few people climbed the minaret and leaped to their death, just like that, out of sheer joy. People went

crazy on that day, it's hard to imagine the stupidities some subjects are capable of committing.

"The next day the king gave the command to tear down an entire neighborhood and build a palace with a garden and fountain for his son. The people who lived in the small cottages wept and begged for mercy, but the soldiers whipped anyone who had not left his cottage by sunset. Hundreds of weeping people who had lost their homes made their way to the palace to plead for help, but the guards only pushed them back. That's the funny thing about happiness: it can turn to unhappiness quicker than the flicker of an eyelash."

"Nicely put!" raved Mehdi and Musa.

"But there was one person who wasn't crying, and that was the witch Mira. Known throughout the land for her kindness, she was also feared for her vindictiveness. She, too, was required to give up her cottage to make way for the prince's palace. When the guards saw Mira, they were afraid and hurried to tell the king that the witch wanted to submit her complaint. The king just roared with laughter: 'Complaint? What is there to complain about? A prince has been born! From now on my entire realm has no more worries! I will not hear any complaints!'

"When Mira the witch heard the king's words, she looked upon the crying people, then turned to heaven and uttered several unintelligible phrases. The blue skies suddenly thundered, the people became frightened and fled. 'O vile king,' screamed the witch, 'for as long as you shall live, you shall never hear another word!' With these words, Mira the witch vanished into thin air, never to return.

"The king was in the midst of an audience with scholars and traders who had come to offer their congratulations when his face suddenly became twisted with pain. He grabbed his head and screamed out loud, 'My ears! My ears!' Then he spun around three times and fell to the ground unconscious. From that day on, the king was unable to hear. But even that hardly worried him, so happy was he to have a son.

"The king continued to rule with a strong hand. He sent hundreds of spies throughout his kingdom to be his ears. They would repeat their reports over and over until the king was able to read the most important details from their lips.

"The stars stood in the young king's favor. Year after year, the heavens provided the farmers with rain for their fields and warmth for their fruits, and the kingdom thrived. But instead of enjoying the peace, the king built up his army and moved to annex a small neighboring realm—it didn't take much to fan the flames of his greed. And no matter how often the soothsayers and scholars warned against such actions, he read less and less from their lips, and he refused to follow their advice. He did exactly as he wanted.

"And in fact, he managed to achieve a great victory

in his first war—because he was a brilliant tactician. His army consisted of fifty thousand soldiers armed with lances and swords, twenty thousand archers, ten thousand knights, and over fifty catapults. The king hid the majority of his troops in the forest and marched on to meet the enemy. When he saw the great army assembled in the plain, he positioned his archers behind the hill, as if he were preparing to attack the enemy's left flank. Then he rode into the middle of the field, wheeled around and fled without even engaging in combat. His opponents saw him fleeing with a tiny army, and scrambled after in pursuit, abandoning all caution. Their best knights chased after the king in great disarray. The king and his retinue soon made it back to safety, and then the skies were darkened with the arrows of his archers. Many horses and many men fell to these arrows . . ." The minister went on at great length about this battle, omitting not a single stroke of the sword, stab of the lance, or blow of the club—just as if he were in court.

"So what happened with the kingdom?" Tuma interrupted.

"After seven years of good fortune, a terrible drought befell the kingdom and caused great suffering. The king's viziers brought him the news, but he refused to read their lips. His subjects began to curse him whenever he appeared on the balcony. But he

mistook their angry fists for friendly waves and replied with his own friendly greetings.

"The drought raged for three long years, bringing misery and tears to the kingdom. But the king was impervious to all such cares, so happy was he about his son, Ahmad. The boy was a wonderful poet and played the lute like an angel. At the age of twelve he could outride all the king's knights and outshoot all his archers. Braver than a panther, the young prince wrestled with the lions the king kept in his palace—no on dared to imitate him. Only water seemed to frighten him. Whenever the sons of the ministers played in the lake, Prince Ahmad sat on the shore and watched the romping boys."

"I know what's going to happen. I know!" laughed Isam.

"Whether you know or not, keep it to yourself. I don't like it when someone kills a story right in the middle," the barber scolded, and Isam hushed him down with a wave of his hands.

"Musa's right. Besides, the story gets even funnier," Faris promised.

Junis wanted to say he didn't find the story funny at all, but he still had hopes it might turn out to be a good one.

"Well, when the granaries were almost empty, the king decided to invade a second neighboring country. This time he had all the slaves in his kingdom

armed with light weapons and sent them to wear down the enemy, after which his real army . . ."

Once again the minister recounted the ruler's war in great detail. Although he appeared to be critical of the king, Faris certainly enjoyed his wars. He described each phase of every battle exactly, how the heads rolled just like that and how the warriors shouted with all their might to strengthen their courage. The minister went on and on, embellishing every action and every movement of the king in such detail that even his close friend Musa joined Ali, who had long since been snoring, and likewise drifted off.

"And what happened to the prince?" Tuma tried to help the minister resume the thread of his story.

"Although he had already turned thirty, the prince seemed disinclined to marry. Meanwhile, the king's lust for plunder led him to launch the famous Five Years War . . ." And here the minister again launched into a battle. By now Tuma was no longer listening —despite the minister's constant assurances that the story would get even funnier. Salim yawned and wished the minister would soon finish. Isam and Junis glared at Faris; they were ready to kill him. Only the teacher interrupted from time to time to exclaim, "What a beautiful turn of phrase."

"And what became of the drought?" asked the barber, when he woke up a little before ten-thirty.

"The drought? It raged for three long years, bringing misery and tears to the kingdom, but the king's

wars had brought him much booty . . ." And the minister proceeded to describe every gem and diadem as carefully as a jeweler taking inventory of his stock. Mehdi continued to praise Faris' beautiful formulations until about half past eleven, when he, too, finally dozed off. Only Salim held his ground, all the time regretting his obligations as a host.

The minister paused, looked at the sleeping guests, and all of a sudden shouted: "And now for the end!" Just as if the cock had crowed, the old men all woke up, sat straight in their chairs, and paid great attention in the hope they would soon be able to go home.

"As I told you, the king reigned for forty years and never listened to anybody. He rarely left his palace, and when he did, his bodyguards beat anyone who dared to come near him.

"One day the king was celebrating his victory over another sultan. This war had been—"

"Enough wars, where's the end of the story? What happened while this goddamned butcher was celebrating?" Junis interrupted angrily.

"Well, he was celebrating his victory. But his subjects had gathered in front of his palace to heap their curses on the king and his ancestors, and to mourn the loss of their sons. After the king had had a bit to drink, he ordered his servants to bring a tray laden with silver coins. He staggered out onto the balcony, grabbed a handful of coins, and flung them into the crowd. But his hand shook so, that most of the coins

landed on the balcony by his feet. As he attempted a second throw, his bodyguards bent down to pick up the coins that had fallen, and for the first time in forty years the king stood before his subjects unprotected. An arrow came flying quicker than the flicker of an eyelash and pierced the royal heart."

"That was nicely said, may God bless your tongue," the teacher commented.

"And yours," replied the minister. "As I said, the bodyguards had only stooped down for a second, to pick up the coins, but by the time they stood back up, the king lay dead on the ground.

" 'The king is dead!' cried the ministers: 'Long live the king!' The subjects shouted with joy. Well, the witch had cursed the king for as long as he should live, and so his ears had gone unused for over forty years. Now, you know, inside the mother's womb, the ears are the first to open a window to the world, and they are the last to close their shutters. Long after eyes, lungs, heart, and brain have passed away, the ears go on hearing, and if someone hasn't strained his brain with too much use while still alive, then when he's dead, not only can his ears hear but his brain can even understand what's being said. Now, the king had more than enough brain left, and his ears were just like new. So he could hear his subjects rejoice and was horribly enraged.

" 'Just look at him lying there, the idiot,' the king

heard his jester say. Oh, how he wanted to box the impudent man's ears, but his hand was long dead. The fool made fun of his master's stupidity, and the ministers all laughed. The king wanted to kick each one of them in the rear, but his legs, too, were long dead.

"Suddenly everything around him grew quiet. The king listened full of curiosity. In the distance he could hear footsteps. 'Quiet!' whispered the fool, 'the queen and the prince are coming.' The jester almost choked trying to contain his laughter.

" 'How did it happen?' the queen sobbed, 'I had only stepped out for an hour, I was sitting with the prince in the garden, and now . . .'

" 'We always told his majesty he should never show himself, but as you know, O queen, he never listened to us. We always told him to keep his bodyguards well fed, so they wouldn't turn around or bend over for anything. But as you know, O queen, he never listened to us, and besides, he paid them so little. The bodyguards bent over to grab the coins—Who wouldn't have? And right at that moment he was hit by an arrow. If my heart had been in my hand, I would have held it in front of his.'

"The king recognized the voice of his minister for internal affairs, who just a moment ago had been laughing himself crooked along with the others. 'Hypocrite,' thought the king—that much thinking he could still do.

" 'And what about me?' Prince Ahmad said. 'How often have I wished to speak with him.' The king noticed a certain peculiarity in the voice of his beloved son, and it wasn't just the sound of intense grief —which, if truth be told, the king was sincerely happy to hear. No, there was an unusual gentleness, a tenderness that made the king a little uneasy. The prince sobbed. 'He loved me for what I wasn't. There have been so many times when I tried to tell him the truth. There have been so many times when I tried to tell him that I am a woman. A woman!' The king listened closely to the voice of his prince, and he heard the cry of a wounded soul. 'A woman!' the king again heard the prince cry out. The king wanted to shut his ears, but he couldn't. 'All of you hated him, but I loved him. For thirty years I lived just for him. And for thirty years I wanted to tell him that I went into the lions' cages only out of love for him, to entice a smile from his tired face. Again and again I invented the ugliest lies to turn away good women who were presented to me so I might choose a wife. Again and again I hoped, out of love for him, that he would die before he discovered the lie of his life, but this morning I resolved to let him live with my truth. I hated always wishing his death. And now, just when I was coming to tell him the truth, he's dead. He cannot hear me,' Ahmad sobbed.

"But the king heard Ahmad very well, and he felt a pain he had never felt while he was still alive. It wasn't worry about the throne, and it wasn't shock at his daughter's revelation. No, it was because he wanted so much to tell his daughter that he did hear her, and that he understood, but his mouth was long since dead. So great was his pain, however, that two huge tears escaped from his dead eyes and slowly rolled across his cheeks. That is my story and I wish you all a long life."

"May God keep your health," the barber answered, looking very pale, while Ali quickly buried his face in his hands.

"What a poor wretch this king was, after all!" sobbed the locksmith.

Salim walked over to his friend, held him by the shoulders, and slowly rocked the big man back and forth, to free him from the story and fetch him back to the little room on Abara Street.

After a while, Ali recovered his composure. "I'm fine now, thank you," he whispered to Salim. The minister stroked Ali's knee and looked at him sadly. "I'm also scared of dying," he said in a voice that could barely be heard.

"Shall I lay out a card for you?" Isam joked with the silent locksmith. But Ali didn't answer.

Faris was the first to get up. He shook Ali's hand for an unusually long time. "You are the ace and the

master of the last night," he encouraged
the old locksmith. "We'll see about
that," Ali grumbled
as he went
out.

12

*Why
Salim was sad
after giving birth
to a beautiful story*

It was past midnight by the time the guests went home. But Salim was wide awake. Inside the small stove, the wood was quietly crackling. Faris' story had begun sadly and ended sadly—what torment the king must have suffered during his last hour on earth!—but as far as Salim was concerned, the minister had spoiled its heart. He had told it so badly that Salim couldn't remember exactly what the middle of the story looked like—despite the fact that he had the memory of a camel. Salim wondered: "Did I nod off like Musa and Ali?" He didn't know for sure.

It's true that Faris had chosen a very difficult story. You can't tell a story about someone who doesn't want to listen and make it sound funny. Salim thought and thought: How should such a story be told?

He kept getting up and feeding wood to the stove, in order to drive the icy cold from his room. His thoughts wandered into the depth of time and the faraway of exotic lands he had always told about. A howling wind swept over the rooftops. All of a sudden he heard two stray cats snarling in the dark. They were fighting. A tin washbowl fell crashing to the ground and the cats ran away in fright. The clatter echoed a few times in the large courtyard. Then the quiet returned. And as if it no longer wanted to disturb the sleeping, the wind abated into a gentle breeze.

Salim's eyes grew wide. Suddenly the story was there, one he had thought up over fifty years ago. He had never told it, and so it had slumbered in his heart all these years. It had first come to him in Great Horn Gorge, when he had cracked his whip and heard it echo off the canyon walls. And now it came back.

Once upon a time—Salim listened to the voice of his memory—there lived a king who didn't know how to listen. Whenever his subjects came to him, he would interrupt them after the first sentence and shout, "Enough! I believe you! Guard, give this man a thousand gold liras!" Or: "Enough, I don't believe you. Guard, give him eighty lashes and take him away!" What he said depended on his mood. He did not want to listen, and because he didn't listen, he was also unjust in dispensing mercy. One day the court jester came to him. The king was in a good mood and asked his fool to tell a story.

The jester sat down at the king's feet and spoke: "I was told, O mighty king, that in earlier times, long before man walked on the earth, in the country of demons, may God protect us from their wrath, there lived a demon and his wife who roamed from canyon to canyon, dwelling in the caves and hollows. Other demons considered him a very poor listener. But his wife suffered more than anyone, because not only did her husband refuse to listen to her, he contradicted everything she said and called it stupid. His ears were completely closed to what her heart was urgently trying to tell him.

"One day she quarreled with him, and when she stood up for herself, he began to beat her. But the worst was that he then insisted on explaining to her, gently and kindly, why the beating was for her own good. His words dripped with honey, but his wife's limbs throbbed with pain. 'You ought to have two mouths instead of one,' she cursed her husband with all her heart, 'and one ear instead of two.' It so happened that at that moment the god of the demons came floating through the canyon. He heard her curse and felt sorry for her. And since he had heard so many bad reports about this demon, he decided to make the wife's words come true. The hard-hearted demon fell into a deep sleep, and when he awoke he discovered that he had two mouths—one above the other—and one tiny ear on top of his forehead, no larger than a chickpea. His old ears lay on his pillow like two shriveled autumn leaves.

"At first the demon was overjoyed and got down on his knees to thank his god for this blessing. Now he could speak faster and louder. From then on he never ceased talking, for even when he ate or drank with one mouth he could still speak with the other.

"The other demons didn't understand the punishment, for now this demon was able to interrupt them even more often, and ask a second question at the same time he was answering the first. And the poor wife, for whom his first mouth had been one mouth too many, was near despair, since now his snoring came rattling out of two.

"More and more the demon heeded only his own two voices, so that his words became an invisible wall that separated him from friend and foe alike. The other demons avoided him like the plague. No one paid any attention to what he was saying. Not even his wife could bear to hear his words. Words, O king, are delicate, magical flowers that blossom only in a listener's ear. This demon's words, however, found no ears at all and wilted the moment they left his lips.

"Soon the demon felt miserable with his dead words. In his loneliness he finally recognized his stupidity, and from then on he practiced penance. He kept both mouths shut and listened better with his one tiny ear than he had with his two large ones. With all his heart he begged the god of the demons to give him a second ear, so that he could hear better. He begged and begged for years. Even his wife felt sorry for him, and his neighbors who dwelt in the nearby hollows, springs, and volcanoes also forgot their anger and begged their creator to pardon the

poor soul. But the god of the demons nursed his wrath for years and barred all supplicants in this matter from his palace. Not until the thousand and first year did he grant the unhappy demon an audience. 'Do you regret your evil deeds?' he asked with angry indignation.

"The demon nodded.

" 'And will you do anything and everything to regain your two ears and one mouth?'

"The demon was willing to make every sacrifice.

" 'Then as of this day, in place of your second mouth you will receive a second ear. But only upon the condition that, until the end of time, you repeat every call and every sentence, whether spoken by demons, animals, or humans. Woe unto you if you should ignore the chirping of even a single cicada.'

" 'Your wish is my command, master of my soul. May the sun and moon be my witnesses: I shall fulfill this condition to the end of time. Please bless me with the second ear,' said the demon, much moved. He began his oath with two mouths and finished it with one.

"To this day the demon roams from canyon to canyon, dwelling in the caves and hollows. And ever since that time he repeats every call and every sentence spoken by demons, animals, or humans. No noise escapes his ears, not even the sound of a rolling pebble."

The jester finished his story, deep in thought.

"And what was the name of this poor demon?" the king wanted to know.

"Echo," answered the fool.

Morning was breaking by the time Salim finished remembering his story. Earlier he had always felt relieved after telling a story, but this time he felt heavy of heart. Why was he so sad? At first he thought it was because the story was too naked and unadorned, stored as it was inside his memory. But no, that wasn't the reason, because that was how he stored all his stories. It was in telling them that he developed his thoughts and clad his bare stories with the appropriate dress and scent and gait. Only bad storytellers retain a story along with all the details. No, what was really burning inside his breast was that there was no one he could tell the story to. In his head, of course, Salim had always known that a story needs at least two people in order to live, but only now did he feel this in his heart.

He placed some wood in the oven and sat down in front of it on the large chair. The flames danced gaily around the wood. They clung softly to its gnarled skin, as if they wanted to caress it. For a moment the wood stayed hard-hearted and cold. It ignored the flames' seduction, but the fire kept sweetly licking its body and tickling its soul with warm poetry. A few splinters and sharp edges, ignoring the warnings of the trunk, dropped their stubborn opposition and finally caught fire. The wood crackled its displeasure, but soon gave up all resistance and started dancing and singing loudly in one great flame. A short while later both wood and flame melted into a quiet whispering glow at rest on a soft pillow of ashes.

When Salim awoke, it was already noon. He jumped up and lifted the blanket from the birdcage. The goldfinch hopped about and rejoiced in the light, drank from its water glass, and let out a loud trill.

Salim was surprised to realize he had spent the entire night on the chair in front of the stove. And he couldn't remember whether he had actually recalled his story, or simply dreamt it.

13

*How
one story's magic
broke two spells and
why seven old men broke into song*

October came with splendid colors—so bright that people forgot it was a harbinger of winter. Wearing its alluring dress, the month managed to slink away just in time, so that it was up to November to deliver the unpleasant news to the people of Damascus, and for the next nine days it was rainy and cold. The farmers were overjoyed when the rain began to patter on their fields. But not the Damascenes, who just moaned and groaned about it being dark and wet. But the tenth day of November dawned so sunny and warm it appeared to have escaped from summer.

Every day has its own soul, so people say, and its own personality: good, bad, boring, exciting—just like people. And some days are loners, who eschew the company of conformists and run away. Who can tell what is really going on inside a summery day that decides to leave July and suddenly pop up in the middle of November, completely unannounced?

On this particular day the sun was radiant above the ancient city. The Damascenes—if they weren't inside their shops and offices complaining about having to work on such a day—came out just to behold the sky, or else to sit in their courtyards, drinking coffee and talking about engagements, colds, and broken gutters. In the middle of the afternoon the street burst into life, as the children released all the energy they had kept pent up during the cold weather—which is why a day like this was likely to see many a broken window.

This afternoon was no exception, and a stray ball shattered a windowpane in the home of the post office clerk Khalil. In the heat of the summer that same broken windowpane would have caused Khalil's wife to curse the ancestors of the perpetrator unto the fourth generation, but now all she did was stand up, call her fifteen-year-old son, hand him money for the repair, and urge him to hurry. Then she sat back down beneath the large lemon tree and continued to drink coffee and gossip—without the slightest trace of anger. In fact, she was laughing heartily half an hour later when one of the children gave away the name of the wrongdoer. The boy's mother was also sitting under the lemon tree. Instead of denying her son's guilt, however, or making light of the broken pane, she apologized for his poor manners—something a mother in Damascus rarely does—and the wife of the postal clerk found the sweetest words in reply.

The beautiful weather lasted until late in the afternoon, when clouds gathered to chase the summer day away—apparently they didn't take well to strangers.

The summer day struggled desperately as the evening weighed more and more heavily upon the bosom of the city.

Salim and his guests were waiting anxiously for the locksmith. Darkness began to fall, and still no sign of Ali. When the clock tower struck eight, every one in the room felt the air begin to crackle. "Where is that man? Only four hours left until midnight of the last day!" proclaimed the minister. He had no sooner finished his sentence when the locksmith entered the room—together with his corpulent wife, Fatma.

"Good evening," Fatma greeted the men, who had frozen in amazement. Then she nudged the barber in the ribs, and after the bewildered man had made room for her, she sat down beside the old coachman as if seeking his protection.

The old men returned the greeting, as propriety demanded, but annoyance oozed from every pore in their faces. It was the first time in over ten years that a woman had joined their circle.

"I've never told a story in all my life," the locksmith explained to his dumbfounded friends, "and my friend Salim knows that better than anyone. When I was little I used to love to talk, and I always wanted to tell stories, but my father warned me: 'Hold your tongue, child, or else it will expose you. With every true sentence you speak about yourself, you grow more naked, bit by bit, and so more open to harm.'

My mother, God bless her soul, always used to add: 'But remember, child, if the conversation does turn to you, never resort to lies. With every lie you weave, the blanket you are hiding under grows bigger, bit by bit, until it finally suffocates you.' Well, since I didn't want to suffocate or come to any harm I've simply never told anything at all, and I don't think I chose to become a locksmith just by chance. Locksmiths don't talk much. It's always so loud in the shop that you have to shout to be heard, so you only say what you absolutely have to.

"Well, I couldn't sleep the whole night. It would be horrible if I left my good friend Salim in the lurch and he lost his voice forever. But I racked and racked my memory and couldn't find a single story. When my wife found out why I was so upset, she told me that she would gladly tell Salim a story."

"I don't know whether the fairy would agree to that," the minister objected. "Didn't she say the gifts had to come from us, his friends?" he checked with Salim. But the old coachman shook his head in a definitive *no*. Disappointed, Faris wrinkled his forehead and leaned back.

The barber rolled his eyes, the teacher mumbled something, and the café owner looked over at the closed door, as if something there could offer consolation. Only Isam and Tuma the emigrant actually smiled at the woman.

"I came here for Salim's sake—I'm not sitting in your court, Excellency, for you to pass judgment on my visit," said Fatma, annoyed.

The minister sat up straight in his chair. "Tell your woman," he said to Ali, "that she should mind her speech!"

"And this is supposed to be an educated man?" Ali snorted. "I don't care whether you were a minister or a shoeshine boy, don't you go telling me what to say to my wife," he went on loudly.

"You knocked on his door," Tuma the emigrant came to Ali's aid, "and he who knocks must bear his reception."

"If you're so smart," Musa turned on the emigrant, "then tell me, because now I'm knocking on your door: Why is Fatma the only one allowed to take part in our meeting? Why couldn't my wife . . ."

"Calm down, boy," Isam scoffed at the barber. "Who said she couldn't? Who?"

Now the old men broke into an unholy quarrel. Junis didn't understand why Ali was allowed to bring his wife, either, and he formulated his objection so cleverly that Musa made an even more insulted face. Other old disputes soon resurfaced. Fatma's presence no longer mattered at all; what did matter was why the barber had praised President Nasser as the savior of Syria despite the fact that two nephews of the café owner and a teacher who professed a deep and sincere love for the locksmith's grandchildren had been sitting in jail for months without the slightest guilt.

Fatma just shut her ears, took out her tin of tobacco, and carefully rolled a very thin cigarette.

Suddenly her mother was at her side, a midwife named Leila, who during her lifetime was known and feared. People said the most amazing things about her magical hands, with which she had brought many of the neighborhood children into the world. But the things they said about her magical stories were even more extraordinary.

No one dared make an enemy of her, for not only could Leila interpret dreams and stars, she was also adept at concocting poisons. Her unknown origins seemed spooky, mysterious, and her sudden disappearance even more so: for no one had laid eyes on her since the day of her daughter Fatma's wedding—it was as if she had dissolved into thin air. Only Fatma knew more, but she guarded this knowledge as her innermost secret.

"Daughter," this wise woman had told her when they parted, "you should know I'm not one of you. I put up with Damascus for eighteen years, until you grew up. And now you have found a good companion—Ali has a good heart. But don't forget: if you want him to listen to you, talk to him now, tell him all your stories, for men understand best while they are in love." Fatma's mother then walked away, ignoring all her daughter's pleas to wait just one more hour, until Ali returned from the mosque, to tell him goodbye. "Why goodbye?" asked the mother. "I'm leaving *you* behind. You are a part of my soul," she added, kissed her daughter, and left.

But Fatma couldn't bring herself to tell Ali any stories—neither on that first night nor in the next few days, nor in the days and years that followed. Ali seemed to her a little hard of hearing, and he rarely ever spoke, not even during their first night. She felt how much he loved her and how much he desired her. But he never said so. In general, he only said what was absolutely necessary, and that succinctly and quietly.

Fatma looked at the crabby old men snapping away at each other. What a brouhaha these old grandfathers were making just because she wanted to tell a story! And her Ali . . . the look on his face when she told him that morning that she could tell Salim not one but fifty stories! "Can you do it well enough?" he had asked her. "Why don't you first tell it to me, so that I can hear whether your story is worthy of my friends." That's right, "worthy"! He, who had no idea about telling anything, was acting like the master hakawati, wanting to test her, the daughter of Leila.

But it's also true that she herself had become less and less talkative over the years. While every new birth had brought new life into the house, instead of speaking more to each other, Fatma and Ali said less and less. Her sister, Rahima, reported the same thing, and her husband, unlike Ali, was the talkative type. Why is it that people tell fewer stories to each other the longer they're together, and not more? Fatma thought about it. Then she remembered her mother's words from fifty years before. "That's it," Fatma whispered to herself, "married couples talk to each other less and less because they're no longer in love."

As a matter of fact, just a few years into the marriage, Fatma had even started to stammer whenever Ali came back from the shop—yet she spoke easily with children or neighbors. She was always afraid he would find her stories silly. It was different with Salim. Whenever he visited she never stuttered; she always knew how much he liked her stories.

Salim interrupted her thoughts to hand her some peppermint tea. She looked up, took the tea, and followed the quarrel with obvious disinterest. The faces of the old men were sour and severe.

"I'm going to drink my tea and go," said Fatma. "You must forgive me for saying that your reception is not worthy of my story. You can't tell anything to people with faces as twisted as yours." Fatma closed her eyes. "No!" she said very quietly. "By the soul of my mother, if you don't come right out and beg me for the story then I am going to leave."

Ali trembled: he had never heard Fatma use such a harsh tone. Salim, on the other hand, beamed, as if Fatma's words were a bouquet of a thousand and one flowers. He stood up and kissed her on the forehead. This was the first time the coachman had ever kissed her in over fifty years of friendship, and his cheeks glowed when Isam said, "Ah, if only I were Salim! If Fatma would accept a kiss like that from me I would be prepared to go for a year without saying a thing."

Ali smiled, relieved.

"Well . . . if it will help Salim, I have nothing against it," the minister—the chief dissenter—finally said, smiling. The teacher, the barber, and, lastly, Junis followed suit.

"Well let's get on with it," Isam bellowed.

"May all quarrels be damned in the grave. It's already half past nine," added Tuma.

Fatma declined to gloat over her victory, and in the ensuing moments just sipped her tea in peace and quiet.

"Tell us your story, please!" begged the barber.

"I will tell you all a beautiful story about the Egyptian witches," she said, and a shy smile briefly adorned her face.

"It's up to us, if I may observe," the teacher grumbled, "to decide whether it's beautiful or not."

"Would you be quiet!" Isam shouted at the teacher.

"I will tell it so that you may be cured, Salim, and so that it may give you joy. God grant a long and happy life . . . only to him who listens well," Fatma continued. "Many many ages ago there was a very smart witch named Anum. She lived in ancient Egypt long before the first mummies and pyramids. She was the first woman allowed to study with the great priest Dudokhnet and learn alchemy, beer brewing, and papermaking. When the priest lay on his deathbed, he named Anum as his successor—'For,' so he explained to the priests gathered around him, 'she alone will succeed in finding the philosopher's stone—' "

"I know this story," the minister interrupted. "First the pharaoh refuses but then assigns Anum seven difficult tasks. And she solves all seven, right?"

"Yes," answered Fatma.

"And does she find the philosopher's stone?" Isam wanted to know.

"Yes she finds it," the minister said. "And whoever so much as licks a particle of its dust becomes a genius, right? The pyramids were built by architects who swallowed a tiny pearl of it, no bigger than a lentil. The bees used to smear their honey everywhere before the Egyptians taught them to use wax for honeycombs and . . ."

Salim shook his head angrily and glared at the minister. Faris halted and turned to Fatma. "Oh, I beg your pardon! I interrupted you!"

"No matter," said Fatma, but the old coachman tasted gall in her voice. "Your Excellency may know this tale, and a hundred others, but no one on this earth has heard the following story, not even my Ali. So either listen or let me go home!"

"For God's sake!" the barber cried out. "Tell it, please, Fatma, tell it!"

"Once upon a time there was a young woman whose name was Leila. She herself was neither beautiful nor ugly, but her tongue was blessed, just like our Salim's tongue has always been and hopefully will soon be again.

"In any case, Leila lost her parents at a young age and from then on lived with her grandparents in a mountain village in the north of Yemen. Even as a little girl Leila loved hearing stories, and whatever she heard once she kept in her heart forever. Nothing in the world could make her forget a story. Well, while the other young women made themselves up every day and sauntered over to the village well, ever on the lookout for men, Leila's only interest was her stories. The strongest man in the village was less attractive to her than a tiny fable, and the most handsome man could not possess her heart even for the length of a brief anecdote. Leila spared no effort to hear a new tale, even if it meant days of travel across dangerous mountains and treacherous steppes.

"In any case, the years passed, and Leila became the best-known storyteller far and wide. On those evenings when she told stories, not only did she charm her listeners, she herself was charmed by what she told. She could speak with stars, animals, and plants as if she were the magic fairy of her own stories. People said that her words had so much power that one day she talked to a rotten tree trunk about spring for such a long time that it sent forth new shoots of green. But Leila didn't just tell her stories to people, animals, and plants, she also confided them to the wind and the clouds. One time there was a drought—and believe me, it was merciless. The farmers prayed and prayed, but not Leila. She climbed the highest mountain and waited there until she saw a little cloud moving quickly across the sky. Leila began to tell the cloud a story, and it stopped to listen. Other clouds joined it, and soon the whole sky was overcast. As the story grew more exciting, the clouds grew darker, and when the story reached its most suspenseful moment, Leila broke off, turned to the clouds, and called up: 'If you want to hear the rest, you'll have to come down here!' The clouds flashed their lightning and rushed down as a sudden shower, just to be closer to Leila."

Fatma paused and finished her cigarette. "Well, there was one summer when it was raining so hard that the people were scared. The earth became sodden, and the swallows hid in their nests on the high cliffs. Late in the afternoon the dogs started howling strangely. When the sun went down, the villagers heard cries for help and shouts of pain coming from a deep grotto not far off. A few of the bravest men and women approached the cave, but they trembled with fear at every cry.

" 'It must be a monster,' said the village elder.

"'A monster? Then why is it crying for help?' an old farmer wondered.

"'Maybe those are the cries of the people it's eating!' presumed a midwife.

"'Or else the monster is trying to lure us in. My father told me that the crocodiles along the Nile hide in the high cattails and cry aloud like a small child until some mother, washing at the river, hears the cries and runs to the place where she thinks a child has fallen into the water. But that's just what the crocodile is waiting for . . .'

"'My grandfather told me hyenas sometimes sneeze—' a shoemaker wanted to confirm.

"'Crocodiles this and hyenas that,' a knight interrupted, 'a true Yemenite must always be prepared to sacrifice himself to answer a cry of distress.' He took his lance and hurried inside the rocky cave, but the only thing to come back out were more cries for help.

"During the day the cave was quiet, but night after night the villagers heard the anguished cries begging for mercy. Grown-ups didn't dare go near the hole, but curiosity drove the children there.

"Two children disappeared in the first week, a girl and a boy. The farmers were convinced that the monster had drawn them into his lair and devoured them. More and more children followed. Although none of the farmers had laid eyes on the creature, whenever they talked about the monster they would describe every tooth in its mouth and every spike on its tail. After a month no one dared mention the word *monster*; they just referred to 'the thing in the hole.' "

Fatma paused, took out her tin of tobacco, and carefully rolled another very thin cigarette.

"That's just like it is today," said Isam, who could no longer bear the silence. "When someone's been arrested we say that he's been 'taken to his aunt's.' And of course we call the prime minister Abdul the Chicken-Eater."

"I thought he was Abdul the Money-Slurper," said Ali.

"No, that's passé," Faris interjected and laughed. "Today my son called him Monsieur Abdul Goose-liver, since he enjoys having that famous pâté flown in from Paris."

"I like that," Isam again spoke up, "and the minister of the interior's called 'The Drum' since he's just as loud and empty."

"In any case," Fatma began again and took a drag on her cigarette, "whenever anyone mentioned 'the thing in the hole,' the farmers would call out: *'Auzu billah min al-Shaitan al-Rajim,'* to protect themselves from the devil.

"One day Leila awoke from a strange dream, put on her clothes, and parted from her grandparents with the words: 'I'm going where my dream has called me. In my dream I saw the thirty children who have disappeared. They were laughing at the entrance to the cave. It's time their laughter returned to the village. Please, don't cry, my dreams will never lead me to my ruin.'

" 'Auzu billah min al-Shaitan al-Rajim!' the grand-parents called out in unison.

" 'Please,' Leila said, 'I want to go. Don't worry, my thousands and thousands of stories will protect me.' She hurried out, and a flock of children followed her to the entrance of the cave. Leila gave them one last look, waved to them, and walked inside.

" 'Leila's gone inside the cave! Leila's gone inside the cave!'—the children's cries echoed through the streets. The sad news spread from house to house, and before the sun had set it had reached the farthest corner of the village. When darkness fell, the villagers heard the cries for help, and a few claimed to recognize Leila's voice. Neighbors visited her grandparents and sadly expressed their sympathy, and one or two people whispered furtively that their long-held suspicions had been confirmed, namely that the poor girl had been crazy since birth.

"Leila meanwhile saw a small light flickering in the depth of the cave. She walked toward it slowly and wondered at the stone figures crowded around the entrance. No human hand, not even the chisel of time could have sculpted people more true to life than those statues frozen in flight. Not a single buttonhole, not a single hair, not even a single bead of sweat was missing from the stone figures struggling to reach the opening of the cave.

"Inside the cave it was so still that Leila could hear her heart beating. After a while she came to a large hall. Here, too, there were stone figures standing all around, facing the hall, frozen in fear. Large beeswax candles were burning everywhere, and in one corner there were more than ten beehives. Across from that was a spring; the water flowed out of one crevice and into another. The bees were buzzing and flying through a hole in the rock out into the open air. Leila saw no trace of a monster. She began to search the cavern for secret entryways—when all of a sudden she stumbled across the horrible creature. May God protect us all from its sight! There it was, lying in a stone trough.

"Leila quickly hid herself behind a rock pile. She didn't have to wait long; an hour after sunset the monster awoke. It looked so frightful I'd better not describe it to you; otherwise I would spoil your evening. The monster licked some honey and bewailed its horrible fate.

"Leila felt her legs begin to buckle with fear, so she closed her eyes for a minute and borrowed the courage of a wounded mother lion from a story she had kept well preserved inside her memory. This mother-courage could make even the strongest warriors tremble.

"Slowly she opened her eyes, and although the walls of the cave shook frightfully with every cry the monster made, Leila's legs were no longer weak. She stood up and with sure steps approached the monster, which looked at her in astonishment, then buried its face in its hands and said, 'Go away, or else I will devour you, go!'

" 'Salaam aleikum! I will gladly listen to your story, but I will not follow your command. I didn't come here to run away!' Leila said and took another step in the direction of the monster.

" 'Leave, for I am cursed and damned, and whoever touches me will turn into a beast!' the monster begged Leila.

" 'That's not true, or else I would know a story about it,' answered Leila, and she touched the monster's slimy paw that was covered with green scales. 'Tell me your story,' she pleaded.

" 'How can I! Every word of my misfortune weighs like a mountain on my breast. Every syllable cuts like a knife. When I want to pronounce it, it rends my throat,' the monster groaned and wept.

" 'Then I'll tell you a story. If it doesn't help you, it may at least relieve your sorrow.' Leila then told the monster the story of the seven sisters.

"The story is long, very long, my noble listeners," said Fatma to the old men who were hanging on her every word. "There's not enough time tonight, but I promise to tell it to you another time. In any case, when Leila described what trials and tribulations the first and oldest sister had been forced to undergo before she finally found happiness, the monster calmed down. Instead of crying, it was listening. Shortly before dawn it laid its head in Leila's lap, taking in her every word, just like a child. The monster was so peaceful that Leila thought it was sleeping. She paused, only to catch her breath, but the creature whispered to her, full of concern, 'And then what did she do to escape from her prison?' Leila gave a tired smile and went on. Noon came, and night, and still Leila continued her story, and whenever she paused to catch her breath the monster begged her to keep on telling.

"Not until the sun stood at its zenith on the second day did the monster fall asleep. Leila lay his head on a stone and walked over to the well. She refreshed herself with the cool water and crept out of the cave unnoticed. Once outside she took off her dress and filled it with pomegranates, figs, grapes, and corn from the nearby fields, then hurried back to the cave. She ate as much as she could, slept just enough to restore her strength, and then waited for the monster to wake up. Then she told him about the sorrows and fortunes of the second sister. Night came and again the new day broke, and the monster listened like a child to the story until it fell asleep. For seven nights Leila held the monster spellbound with her stories. It did not shed another tear.

"On the seventh night, the seventh and youngest daughter fell into disgrace with her ruthless father, who was a king, and the stern judge pronounced the royal sentence: the daughter would be beheaded the next day at sunset if no one could be found who would take her place and sacrifice himself. At this point the monster started up, excited.

" 'But there was no one,' Leila spoke on, very moved, 'who wanted to give up his life to save the youngest daughter.'

" 'But I want to!' the monster suddenly cried out: 'She is innocent. I will gladly give my life so that she may live!'

"When the monster spoke these words, its skin split with a resounding clap and a handsome youth stepped out of the shell. He was as beautiful as dew on the petals of a rose. His noble offer to sacrifice himself had proven stronger than the spell that had bound him. 'I am Prince Yasid,' he said, looking deep into Leila's eyes. 'You have freed me from my torment and I shall grant whatever your heart desires.'

"Suddenly Leila and the prince heard hundreds of children giggling. The boys and girls who had been turned to stone were released from their spell together with the prince and were now laughing at him because he was stark naked. The children who had been frozen in flight were also released. They heard the laughter in the cave and came running in to look. After a while they all went back to the village and reported that a naked youth was living in the cave, and that he was very shy and that he had turned red because he was naked. Leila was well; she was taking a bath in the cool water while the youth was grilling some ears of corn for her over a small fire. The parents of the missing children danced for joy, and the whole village went wild with glee.

" 'Of all the friends who followed me,' the youth told Leila, 'these bees are the only ones who stayed. They gave me light and honey. All the others succumbed to fear at the sight of me—except for you—and so they turned to stone. But let me tell you my story from the beginning. You will hardly believe it.

" 'My father, King Yasid the First, ruled over a happy Yemen for more than twenty years. On the day of my birth, he had a dream . . .' And Prince Yasid told Leila his truly unbelievable story. He went on for three days. In any case, there's not enough time to tell this story to you now, but if I live long enough, I will be happy to tell it to you some other time. As I said, the youth told her his story, and when he had finished, he made his way outside with Leila. People had been waiting anxiously in front of the cave for days, for they had heard whispers and laughter coming from the belly of the grotto, but no one had dared to set foot inside.

"Yasid addressed the crowd: 'Salaam aleikum, kind grandparents, neighbors, and friends of this storyteller who has freed me from the curse, so that the words from my heart, which have sought the light of the world for so long now, fly to it like butterflies.' The farmers shouted with joy.

" 'I hereby declare,' Yasid continued, 'as Prince of Sa'na and as the son of King Yasid the First, that I intend to take Leila to be my wife!'

" 'Your wish is our command,' the grandparents stammered in awe.

"The villagers cheered the king and his successor, and the grandparents wept tears of joy. But then Leila raised her delicate hand. 'No, my prince. You are gracious and kindhearted, but it is my wish to venture forth into the world. Your palace is firmly rooted in the earth and will keep me as painfully chained as the scales that tormented you for all these years. Farewell!'

" 'But—' the prince began to express his displeasure.

" 'No *but,* my prince. You promised to grant me whatever my heart desired—or is your word lightly given and lightly broken?' she said and walked away without haste or hesitation. The people looked at her agape. Now many were absolutely certain that Leila was crazy.

"In any case, the prince returned to the capital. He had the treacherous vizier, who had had him changed into a monster, thrown into a dungeon. Out of gratitude he sent seven camels laden with silk, silver, and gold to Leila's grandparents.

"But Leila ventured forth into the world. From the mountains of happy Yemen she traveled across the desert to Baghdad. For three years she lived in the city of the Thousand and One Nights until she met a man and fell in love. He was only visiting Baghdad, for he was an engineer on the Hejaz railroad that ran from Jordan to Mecca and Medina. Leila saw this as a gift from heaven. She traveled with her beloved, and whenever she wanted, she would get off the train, to tell stories and to listen to them in the nearby cities, villages, and Bedouin camps until her lover's train returned. Her fairy-tale happiness lasted for years.

"She became pregnant, but Leila was like the gazelles that continue leaping about right up to their labor. Her beloved was happy that she was pregnant and even happier that he was promoted. He was named station superintendent, and he joyfully informed Leila that from then on he would no longer have to move around. But she just broke into tears. That same night she fled to Damascus, where she brought a daughter into the world. She named her daughter Fatma. And while a prince, a kingdom, and her beloved all had failed to keep this wonderful storyteller in one place, Leila's love for her daughter bound her to Damascus for eighteen years during which time she earned her living as a midwife. One sad day she came to her daughter . . ." Fatma paused, wiped away a tear, and blew her nose into her large handkerchief. "She said she could no longer stay and that for years she had been dreaming of telling stories in faraway cities and villages. Her daughter was dumbfounded. She had only seen the mother in Leila and not the magical storyteller. 'You've grown old. Stay here,' the daughter begged, 'Ali and I will take care of you!'

" 'Old?' Leila shouted and laughed. 'Good story-tellers are like good wine—the older the better!' And she left, together with her thousands and thousands of stories."

"I've never heard a story like that in all my life!" Salim cried out in his deep voice. Then he stood up and again kissed Fatma on her forehead.

Outside, above the roofs of the old town, it was thundering. But a great silence reigned inside the room until finally the men broke out into a roaring song. They sang so badly and so loudly that even the goldfinch woke up and began to hop inside its cage and squeak at an unusually shrill pitch.

The noise in the room was so loud that the neighbors who lived in the same building and in the houses nearby woke up, quickly threw on their robes, and hurried to the old coachman.

14

Why
because of Salim
I tumbled to the ground and
a swallow sailed into the skies

It's been thirty years, but to this day I am convinced that back then no one on our street knew whether the old coachman had really lost his voice or whether he had simply duped the whole neighborhood.

Salim was my friend. He told me everything, even the thoughts he had during those three months. That's how I heard the echo story. And I was very proud that I was the only one he told about his unique discovery, that you can taste voices with your ears. But every time I asked him if he had really lost his voice or whether he had only been pretending, he would simply reply with a crafty smile.

I remember one day in 1963. School was closed on account of the coup on the eighth of March and we were idling about in the street. That year spring seemed to be in a rush; its warmth chased us outside, although one of the neighbors, a young woman, had died the day before. Out of respect for her family we were not allowed to run around or play music or do anything that would make noise. At some point the conversation turned to Salim. One of the boys in the neighborhood had the gall to claim that he knew for a fact that the old coachman had made fools of his seven friends and all his neighbors. What's more, Salim had supposedly confided this to him in friendship.

I was boiling with rage. Today I realize that for a while I believed his boasting. I felt betrayed by Salim since he hadn't told his secret to me. Well, then this so-called friend of Salim's suddenly shouted out loud, for all to hear, "And I'll tell you something else, Salim is a miserable cheat."

The boy was built like a tank. I, on the other hand, was very small, but that never stopped me. "Listen, you jackass," I cried, "it's only out of respect for the soul of our neighbor that I don't knock you down right here, but if you're as brave as your mouth is big, then please be so kind as to meet me on the field."

The colossus was so kind, and the boys were happy about this new distraction. Quietly we left the street.

When we reached the field, I discovered that my rage had dulled a bit, and that my reason, the mother of fear, had grown a little more alert. And there the boy was, right in front of me, standing with his arms crossed and his feet apart—a mountain of flesh with a crooked smile.

"Maybe that sentence of yours just slipped out. It happens to all of us on occasion," I said to the boy, as a way of saving face—and also to avoid a fistfight I was sure to lose.

"Slipped out?" he bellowed. "Not only is Salim a miserable cheat, he's the son of a whore six times over."

I slugged him with all my strength. The colossus staggered backwards. He was dumbfounded. He looked me over for a moment, then came at me like a steamroller and knocked me down without the slightest effort. Even so, I managed to pull myself together, and the boys had to hold us apart. My nose was bleeding but still I kept yelling at the big boy with all the fury I could muster: "And don't you forget it! Any time you insult Salim, I'm going to box your ears." I must have seemed pretty comical, because the colossus was just rolling on the ground with laughter. Then he tried to hug me.

But I went home grumbling and cursing Salim in my heart for having caused such unpleasant swellings on my nose and eyes.

Sometime that afternoon our neighbor Afifa whispered something to the old coachman about the fight. As I've said, her tongue was famous. People often joked that even radio announcers started to stutter if she talked during the news.

Salim came running over to me and wanted to know the reason for the fight.

"The reason?" I yelled at him. "For over three years I've been asking you whether you really did lose your voice. Am I your friend or not?"

He laughed. "You're my best friend, even if you

are a little too careless when it comes to tangling with giants."

"I want to know. I couldn't sleep for three months. You have no idea how worried I was for you at the time. Every day I prayed that you would speak. Now, tell me!"

"There you are very mistaken," he replied, "I felt your worry, deep in my heart." Then he laughed with satisfaction, stroked my hair, and said, "But now you don't have to worry anymore. I'm all better!"

Suddenly a child cried out from the courtyard: "Uncle Salim! Uncle Salim! Where are you? A swallow's fallen from its nest! Uncle Salim!"

The old coachman looked down at the courtyard from my room on the third floor. A flock of children was standing around a twelve-year-old boy whom no one knew; they were all looking at Salim with pleading eyes.

"This boy's from Ananias Street," shouted Abdu, Afifa's son—a notorious troublemaker. "We're at war with them, but we allowed him to come to you because he found a swallow on the ground," Abdu added, giving the nervous boy a small poke just for the fun of it.

"That's right, I found it this morning next to the flower pots in the courtyard. It fell out of its nest. But it can't fly anymore and it doesn't want to eat anything. I caught three flies for it, but it didn't even touch them," the boy said in a quiet, sad voice.

"Bring the swallow up here, my boy. And all the rest of you stay in the courtyard and watch," he told the children. Despite Salim's command, Abdu tried to sneak up unnoticed.

"I said all of you!" the old coachman shouted, and the troublemaker stopped short on the landing and watched with envy as the boy climbed up with the swallow.

Salim covered the bird in his large hands and walked onto the balcony. I took the shy boy by the arm and followed the old coachman.

"Heaven! I give this swallow back to you!" the coachman cried out loud and turned slowly in a circle. The children in the courtyard stood on their tiptoes and stretched their necks to follow the ceremony exactly.

"Heaven! I give this swallow back to you!" Salim cried out a second time with an even louder voice and once more turned in a circle. Then he closed his eyes, whispered something to the swallow, kissed it, and paused for a moment. "Heaven! I give this swallow back to you!" Salim launched the swallow into the sky, and up it sailed, uttering a loud call. Then it made a loop around our house as if in parting and raced away.

Salim looked at the boy from Ananias Street. "You're a good lad. Don't be afraid, no one will touch you," he said and turned to Abdu, who was now pacing back and forth in the courtyard like a tiger in a cage.

"Whoever lays a hand on this boy is my enemy. Abdu, you will take him to his street, and if anyone so much as touches a hair on his head, I will never trust you with anything else. Give me your word!"

"I'll guard him like my own eyeball. Cross my heart!" Abdu was exaggerating, but the coachman didn't mind.

"Hurry now, my little one," Salim said to the boy, while Abdu started bullying the other children and boasting that the boy was now under his personal protection.

The old coachman looked at my swollen eye and fat nose and laughed. "You should never tangle with boys who are bigger than you, otherwise you'll never become a storyteller. You have to beat them with your tongue. Do you know the story about the tiny woman who fell into the hands of a giant and outwitted him with her stories?"

"You don't mean Scheherazade?"

"Heavens no! My friend, this is a story that no one knows but me. But since you are my best friend I'll share it with you. I met the woman shortly after her escape, and she told me her very strange and very gruesome tale. Brrr . . . I get goose bumps just thinking about it. You won't believe it. But do you want to hear it anyway?"

"Yes, yes, I do," I answered, brimming with curiosity.

"Then make some tea and come over. I'll be waiting for you!"

When I made my way over with the tea, Salim had just prepared his waterpipe. I sat down with him and listened for two hours to the first of twelve installments of an unbelievably exciting story, which he told me in the days that followed. But the story is very, very long and it won't fit in this book, so I'll have to tell it some other time.

Leabharlanna Poibli Chathair Bhaile Átha Cliath
Dublin City Public Libraries

The Dark Side of Love

'At last, the Great Arab Novel - appearing without ifs, buts,
equivocations, metaphorical camouflage or hidden
meanings ... the book is a compulsive read.'
— *The Independent*

Damascus, 1969: above St Paul's Chapel, a body hangs in a basket over the city wall. The corpse is that of a high-ranking Muslim officer, and soon the Secret Service takes over the case.

But Detective Barudi is not content to let this mystery disappear. Alone, he begins to unravel a clan war that has dominated the lives of three generations. At its heart lies the story of Rana Shahin and Farid Mushtak, two lovers whose struggle to be united must overcome old tribal structures, and their country's history and politics.

The Dark Side of Love is a mosaic of stories; each piece has an individual shape and color, and together they make up a dazzling whole, as the tales of three generations of lovers are set against a century of Syria's turbulent history, in a panoramic view of its religious and political conflicts.

www.arabia-books.co.uk

The Calligrapher's Secret

'The background to this bold and political novel is cosmopolitan: Jews, Armenians, Arabs and Iranians live cheek by jowl in Schami's Damascus. Finely rendered into English by Anthea Bell, *The Calligrapher's Secret* is a celebration of diversity.'
— *Times Literary Supplement*

Even as a young man, Hamid Farsi is acclaimed as a master of the art of calligraphy. But as time goes by, he sees that a weaknesses in the Arabic language and its script limit its uses in the modern world. In a secret society, he works out schemes for radical reform, never guessing what risks he is running.

His beautiful wife, Nura, is ignorant of the great plans on her husband's mind. She knows only his cold, avaricious side. No wonder she feels flattered by the attentions of his amusing, lively young apprentice. And so begins a passionate love story – the love of a Muslim woman and a Christian man.